A Flair for Trouble

A Teachable Cozy Mystery

Kristen Bahls

Book Cover by 100 Covers

Illustrations by HungrydamyArt

first edition 2025

To the best teachers and mentors I know, Jennifer Holcomb and Dr. Cheryl Scott. To mom, thank you will never be enough. To my *Worker Bees* and *Champions at Work*, thank you for making me a better teacher.

Chapter One

Cohen

I suck in a gulp of stale air while straightening my tie for what feels like the fiftieth time in five seconds before giving up and flinging it across the room. What kind of try hard wears a tie on his first day of teaching, anyway? Technically it's a week before students enter the building. I stare at the walls of my computer lab, I wonder if I should find the other teachers, so I don't have to stew in uncertainty. I roll my shoulders back with false bravado and step into the hallway. I hear them before I see them.

The rhythmic pounding of their feet clomp like a herd of elephants as they try not to eat it on the freshly waxed linoleum floor. My shoulders meet my ears, as a sharp squeal is followed by a crash that comes out of nowhere. Before I can get my bearings, I feel the sharp sting of sudden pain as my feet fly out from under me. On the way down, I instinctively hold onto the person I've collided with. Splayed out on the floor, I stare up at the stained ceiling tiles trying to decide if any of the aching is worthy of a hospital visit. I falsely assume the commotion would stop the group of trotting teachers to check on the fallen, but it's every man for themselves today.

I start to get up, the stinging in my knees and back starting to calm a bit, muttering, "What the…" and questioning all the life choices that led me to this moment, when I feel the soft touch of hands patting me down to check for injuries.

"I'm so sorry. Are you ok?" a concerned voice chirps. For the first time I focus on the teacher before me. Her blonde hair falls around her shoulders, pieces askew after the force of the impact when we collided. A blush creeps up her cheeks, highlighting a dusting of freckles. She rights her now wrinkled blazer, and I realize I'm staring. But who wouldn't get lost in her eyes? Which reminds me of bluebonnets. Before I can think better of it, I brush one of the strands out of her face. I quickly realize my faux pas, touching her without permission, and keep my hands trained at my side. Pain temporarily forgotten. "I'm fine, thanks. Why were you running?"

We stare at each other for another awkward beat. Breaking the silence, she says, "Lunch duty rosters are up." As if that's supposed to explain something? She continues, "The good spots fill up fast, and the principals just sent out an email to find them in the library."

Still not understanding why lunch duty is so important, but apparently determined to put my foot in my mouth, I respond with, "Oh. Is this our meet cute?" We start gingerly walking in the direction the others went. We walk in silence for a few seconds longer than comfortable. I can tell I've thrown her off. Incredulously, she says, "Oh, you mean when I tackled you trying to get a lunch duty spot just now? Yeah, I don't think that would qualify as cute." Her spine straightens, and she suddenly seems all business.

Sticking out her hand, she asks, "Cohen, right?" In a daze, I respond with a simple, "Yeah." She winces. "I'm Elle Dannon, your mentor."

I nod, slowly processing the information. Not only did I get mowed down in the hallway, but then I proceeded to hit on my mentor. *Fantastic.*

CHAPTER TWO

Elle

With a shrug, he hesitantly picks up his pace to match mine. Will the assistant principals search the security footage and pull a clip of teachers running down the hall like the promise of Expo markers, tissues, and smaller class sizes await us in the library? Probably. Seriously, they'll make a meme out of anything.

And have we shouted at students for creating the same shoe skid marks from playing tag in the hall on the freshly waxed floors? Yep, but this is lunch duty. And you can't mess around with your lunch, otherwise known as the 30 minutes of peace and quiet as you stare into space, or for me, time to lament about my day with the other teachers. To each their own.

It wasn't rocket science to connect the dots. The new face in the hallway is my new mentee, aka the only new teacher in our department. When they said he'd been in industry before teaching, I assumed that meant he'd be an old dude, but I guess you know what they say about assumptions. Trying to slyly fix my hair while power walking is a challenge. I'm doing my best to match his pace, but with his longer stride I feel like I'm a toddler trailing behind their mom.

Huffing and puffing, I start in on my explanation. Wouldn't want him to think we're crazy.

"They send an email out every year with the duty roster and sign-up is first come, first serve. If you get a duty spot by your classroom, you get a few extra minutes for lunch before you have to walk over, and you want to make sure you don't sign up for a red zone like the middle of the cafeteria," I wheeze. Trying not to breathe hard has the opposite intended effect, and I struggle to exhale air out through my nose, which results in what I'm sure are a few loud gulps.

Cohen takes a beat to respond as the information hits him, and the group slows our pace to a brisk walk as we near the library. "Why? I think it would be entertaining to hear them with their friends outside of class."

I scoff. "Last year, they put a new teacher on that duty, and ten minutes later he was sitting on the floor criss cross apple sauce, crying. It's like if you put all the students you usually separate with seating charts together with free time and food they can throw your way, times the entire cafeteria. I wouldn't recommend it."

"Who knew I would need mentoring already. I'll keep that in mind." He smiles.

I push down the urge to restate the importance of following my advice as we all try to catch our breath. We push open the solid doors with a loud creak and stop in the doorway with a few blinks. The library is relatively empty aside from our group. Suckers.

In an effort to claim the good duty spots while we still can, we race to the sign-up sheets and are greeted by our assistant principal, Ezra. "Wow, how did you guys get here so fast. Is the whole CTE group here?" He chuckles while the only sound from us is the scribble of frantic pens to paper as we all reach over each other in a tangle of limbs to claim our spots. There are only a few slots near our classrooms, making them precious real estate that can easily be taken by the others in our group.

CTE stands for Career and Technical Education classes. They are basically anything that can be considered a vocation or trade from cosmetology to robotics. I can already tell we are one second away from someone in our group making a comment about how we wouldn't have to run down if they just made the sign up digital, but luckily everyone just puts on fake smiles instead.

Jade, my best friend, bumps my shoulder and whispers, "Are you ok? That fall was brutal?"

"You mean collision?" I clarify, nodding subtly to Cohen still standing right next to me.

She nods, stifling a laugh.

She starts, "Sorry, I would have waited but— "

I finish for her, "Lunch duty, I get it."

"But I did sign you up for a slot next to me. Lunch duty buddies again this year." We share a silent high five. Our conversation is interrupted by the sound of a clipboard hitting a hard surface causing everyone in the room to jump.

"Why are there no more spots anywhere good? I can't survive another year in the hallway by the band hall. If I have to hear Hot Cross Buns on repeat for another semester, I will go insane," Dwayne, the robotics teacher laments. Poor guy.

Our wide-eyed AP is silently calculating what to say next and I can tell the poor man is utterly flabbergasted at how so many emotions are tied to lunch duty. Thankfully, our other AP comes to the rescue and is in front of the distraught teacher in a second. While we have multiple assistant principals, two are specifically tied to us and are supposed to know the ins and outs of our classes. Ezra is new and was an English teacher, so he probably thought he had it easy getting the "fun" subjects.

It's not that our classes aren't fun, but imagine teenagers with power tools and explosive gas in Construction or Welding, live animals in AG, knives in Culinary, or electrical cables and heavy equipment in IT and Video Production?

Everyone in our big group sticks around to grab their textbooks from the library storage room while I make the walk back to my classroom solo. My sneakers echo against the floor with each step, giving me time to reflect. This is Wilson High, where I once walked the halls as a student and later landed my first teaching job three years ago. Now, I'm starting the year as a mentor. After my own mentor helped me survive what I'll admit was a pretty rough first year, I knew the moment I hit my three-year mark and became eligible, I had to pay it forward.

The job of a mentor is never done as you are simultaneously a teacher, sounding board, confidant, and therapist. It's your job to try to steer your mentee to foster a love of teaching, veering away from overwhelm and burn out. Teaching is like learning a new language. Everything is foreign at first and you don't know what you're doing half the time, but with experience and practice, everything eventually clicks once you get the hang of it. No matter where you teach, some things are universal in education, like the frustrations of parents and admin, the impossible tasks being added to your plate, and most importantly, the students that burrow into your heart and mind, causing you to dawn your lanyard and unlock your classroom door another day.

I unlock my classroom to see Jade already sitting in my plush white teacher chair, the only item in my room that remains white because it is off limits to students. "Hey, weren't you just at the library? How'd you beat me back?" I ask.

Jade flicks the candle warmer on my desk on and off, before looking straight at me. "Oh, I had one of the first-year teachers get my books for me. They're still in the I want everyone to like me stage, and it wasn't that hard to talk them into it." She halfheartedly chuckles to herself.

Jade and I started the same year and had classrooms within powerwalking distance of each other. Not only are we best friends, but roommates too. Living on a teacher's salary doesn't afford you living alone privileges, but we are lucky to have each other and not have to dip into the pool of random adult roommates.

I narrow my eyes at her. "Jade, are you ok? You don't seem like yourself."

"I'm fine," she says with a huff.

I move closer. "Because the Jade I know would take more pride in her ability to get the first years to do her chores for her." She glares at me in mock offense. "On that note, never be a mentor teacher."

She bats me away. "I'll leave that to you. By the way, I'm going to need to know what you guys talked about on the walk to the library. He stayed pretty close to you in the library."

"Shut up. This is about you." I try to get us back on track.

"Sure, but we will have to go over this later. How'd you get lucky enough to actually have a hot mentee?" Jade whines.

"He's not that hot," I say in defense, but realize I'm fighting a losing battle based on Jade's glare.

"Ok, fine. He's attractive. And looks around our age. But who knows? He could be 40 and just look 25," I lament.

Jade scoffs. "He is not 40. But if you're determined to deny it, then who am I to stop you?"

"I'm shocked you're letting this go," I confess, rubbing my sweaty palms together.

Smirking, she adds, "Wasn't planning on it. So, not that hot means you think he is." She glances down at her nails. "It makes sense, because he is literally your type to a T, buuuuuttt, he's a teacher too?" She laughs to herself before glancing back up at me. "You're not gonna last long."

I huff. "Whatever, didn't you and Parker get together after a few weeks? It's not like you don't flirt with co-workers."

I groan internally, knowing how much she's going to bring this up. There was a barista that flirted with me at a coffee shop we frequented last year, and she had to dissect every interaction. Especially now that she has Parker, she's made it her personal mission to find me a boyfriend.

Jade's boyfriend Parker is perpetually overwhelmed as the basketball coach, senior sponsor, and science teacher. They've known each other almost since we started, but they interacted more last year when they tried to thwart a string of pranks in the school.

I notice a shift in her demeanor as she looks at the floor before quietly stating.

"I have a bad feeling about this year." She waits a beat before continuing, using her fingers to punctuate each point. "Parker didn't laugh at any of my jokes when we Facetimed this morning, so he'll probably break up with me. I had the best roster last year and I don't want new kids. I want to keep the same students another year. And I overheard the AP's talking about a new duty they want to assign us."

Duty is any additional time outside of actual teaching that teachers monitor or chaperone students. This can be lunch duty or our presence at any after school events. Jade has a tendency to catastrophize when she's stressed, but the matching twist in my gut tells me she might not be too far off this time. Still, I know better than to let us spiral down that rabbit hole with so much to get done before the school year starts.

Instead, I answer with, "Remember this time last year?"

Jade scoffs. "I mean..."

I cut her off, "When we were lying on the floor of my classroom."

She chimes in, "Which we'll never do again after the incident with the —"

I shudder and respond, "Never again." Grim smiles slowly spread across our faces in mutual understanding. Moral of the story is to never lie on the carpet. A stray cat had been hanging around over the summer, and after taking a short nap on the floor we got fleas. I feel a phantom itch creeping up just thinking about it.

"But the point is, that we wanted things to stay the same last year: and we ended up having our best teaching year yet," I point out.

"Yeah, you win. I think because so many things are the same year to year; same classroom, same syllabus, same routines, that it feels weird when something seems different. I thought being a teacher meant I could embrace the routine, and not have to change all the time," she huffs.

I get up and pull her into a hug. We cling to each other, and I can't help but feel grateful to have found such an amazing friend and roommate. Jade may appear rough around the edges with her sarcastic nature, but she's intensely loyal and tenacious, stopping at nothing to make herself and others around her better. I have a feeling I'm going to lean on her extra for whatever this year brings.

Chapter Three

Elle

Soreness is already creeping into my muscles from sitting too long at my desk. To combat it, I try to stretch a bit in my chair, determined to finish my lesson plans and then go and check on my mentee. If Cohen, the new graphic design teacher, and I are going to work together, I have to show him he can trust me from the beginning. And he can't trust me if he can't find me, so I need to stop by at least once a day. That's the only reason I plan to visit him. Strictly professional I tell myself as I set my hands back on my keyboard.

I smile, thinking of my mentor Patty, who always brought a Ziploc baggie of homemade cookies each morning. I guess from the first time she laid eyes on me she knew I ate my feelings in chocolate chip cookies. It was more than just the cookies, of course. She cared enough to check on me every day even though she had a to-do list as long as a CVS receipt. Whether you're a first year or forty-year teacher, the tasks never stop coming.

Determined to be the best mentor ever, I can't screw this up. Who knows what he thinks of us after the marathon lunch duty race? I don't do things halfhearted. It's like in high school, I didn't just want the A, I wanted to be the example the teacher kept on display, pulling my crumpled project out of her desk drawer as she went over the directions. Lost in thought, I barely notice the soft knock at my door. I turn to see Cohen leaning against the door jam and a sheepish smile on his face.

My "be the best mentor that ever mentored" plan didn't include a mentee with a strong jawline, perfectly tousled brown hair, and piercing hazel eyes that look like a multicolored marble, which seems like a rookie mistake at this moment. A very distracting mistake. Trying not to stare, I start to break the silence, until he beats me to it.

"Can you believe it?" he says, leaning further into my room.

"Believe what?" I manage to say, trying to determine if I totally spaced out.

"What are the chances the first teacher I meet is my mentor?" Cohen asks, his face brightening.

I twist my hands in my lap. "So we're counting that run in earlier? Do we have to?"

A flash of embarrassment crosses his features. "Yeah, I didn't mean to flirt with you. I'm like that with everyone." He finishes the end of his sentence as if it's a question.

Quickly wanting to diffuse the situation and any lingering awkwardness, I cut him off. "Yeah, I'm sure you are."

A laugh escapes him, and my eyes widen when I realize how that comes across. "No, I didn't mean it like that," I stumble.

I've been told that I don't hide my emotions well, so I'm sure that I'm not subtle as I try to come up with a response, but my brain is blank. This must be how students feel when they're called on and don't know the answer. I make a mental note to immediately stop this practice. Trying to dig myself out, I switch gears in our conversation.

"Did you walk over here for something?" I ask, trying to calm my heart rate. I'm never flustered like this.

"Oh yeah. I was hoping you might be willing to lend me your staple remover?" he says, stepping closer to my desk, maintaining an impressive level of eye contact.

I fish around in my desk and produce the standard black claw shaped staple remover that belongs to every office around the world.

He looks down at it, and huffs out a laugh. "I meant the good kind."

My expression becomes serious as I open the hidden middle drawer in my desk and pull out the pink, flat staple remover.

"Do you promise to return the holy grail of staple removers? This has been with me since day one."

He reaches for it with his right hand and holds out a pinky in solidarity.

"Promise."

We seal the deal with our pinkies, and I'm no longer worried about my staple remover. I try not to blush at the contact. It's just a pinky promise.

"So, how's everything going?" I ask, trying to be nonchalant.

"Pretty good," he says, twirling the staple remover between his fingers.

"I have all my lesson plans done for the first week. I think I have the hang of this whole teaching thing."

My eyes bug out in astonishment, I don't even have my plans done for the first week.

"Maybe you don't even need a mentor?" I question.

"Oh I definitely need a mentor." He continues taking a step forward even closer to my desk, calm as ever.

"Ok. What did you have in mind for the first week?" I ask, trying to deflect.

He pulls a piece of paper out of his pocket, single sided, and hands it to me. It's still warm from body heat as I smooth it out and start reading.

I bite my lip in an attempt to not laugh. It's sectioned out into days of the week and scribbled on each day are bullet points with phrases like, "copyright rules presentation," and "go over syllabus" is on the first day.

I motion to the computer chairs behind him.

"Pull up a chair, we have some work to do on these," I say, waving the paper in my hand.

He grabs a chair and rolls it over.

"That bad?"

"No, it just needs a little bit of work, which is exactly what I'm here for," I say, relieved my mentee hasn't out taught me before the first day of school.

I try to square my shoulders in what I think is a confident gesture, but I end up slamming my elbow on the metal bar of my desk.

Cohen tries to hide his smile at my blunder but fails miserably.

Cohen leaves with a wave and full lesson plans for the first week. With the afternoon to myself, I'm able to put on my favorite true crime podcast and get to work. For obvious reasons, I can't blast a murder podcast when students are in the building, but the predictability of the hosts laying out all the facts that accompany a case put me at ease. I feel like I've listened to so many I could solve one at this point. I'm sure all the other listeners have the same naïve misgivings that they have the skills to find the answers to something as intricate as a murder.

But in my cozy classroom bubble, I can imagine I'm the best teacher/detective that ever lived and get some lesson planning done for the first week. If I've learned anything about professional development week/in-service, there is never enough time to plan in your classroom, so you have to make the most of it.

After a few hours, the information overload has left me in a numb stupor as I slide into the student desk at the front of Jade's room. Admin mandates stated we had to meet today, but at least we had some planning time in our rooms earlier. They want to make the most out of this week even if the days are so packed they feel endless.

I'm video, Cohen is graphic design, and Jade is animation. Since we teach the closest subject matter and our content overlaps, meeting makes the most sense.

They share the same look of utter fatigue as Jade is propping her head up with her fists and Cohen is staring into space, which happens to be level with the glitter lava lamp Jade keeps at the front of the room. Yep, this will be a very productive meeting.

When the clock strikes on the hour, I rise from my spot and hand them the supplied agendas. Cohen looks at his as if it offends him, and Jade's mouth turns down in disgust. "Elle, as much as I love your observance of the rules, I think I speak for all of us when I say we need a break. I just got done with a month of lesson plans. A month and I need a break," she reasons lying her head on her desk.

"Woah, that's amazing." I beam at her. "I probably don't need to remind you, but this is mandatory. Don't worry, I figured this would happen, so let me grab something that I think will help." Without waiting for an answer I make a beeline for my room and grab three cans I have in my desk drawer.

As I make my way back I can hear Jade and Cohen mid conversation.

"And that's why you should never doubt Elle's surprises," she says with a self-assured smile.

I have the cans behind my back as Cohen tries to guess what it is.

"Well now I have to see what magical cure you are gracing us with today." He cranes his neck, but I keep turning to hide them just out of view.

Jade is sitting at the desk with my back to her, so she can see already and is holding out her hands, greedily eyeing the cans. Utilizing my dramatic flare, I tap the cans with my nails, creating a distinctive metal ting.

Cohen's eyebrows raise in disbelief as he guesses. "Wait, did you bring us alcohol?" He looks simultaneously impressed and a little freaked out.

A laugh of disbelief escapes my lips as I hold it out toward him. "Riley, former LAPD detective, and current law enforcement teacher, next door could walk me out of the building in handcuffs if I did that. Alcohol is not allowed on school grounds."

He takes the can from my hand, catching on. "But energy drinks are."

I walk over and set Jade's on her desk as she looks at us through narrowed eyes.

She cracks open the can and takes a long swig, but I know she's going to drill me about Cohen later. Having been friends for so long,

I can see her taking in our easy conversation with scrutiny. It can take me a bit to warm up to people. She eyes us over her can as I decide to keep the meeting moving. Cohen is also quiet as he almost chugs his can in an effort to expedite the surge of energy he needs to get through the day.

I continue, "Before we get further into the mechanics of our curriculum, I want to briefly cover the first day of school games. What did you both have in mind?"

"You know I had to stick with a classic. Human checkers for the win!"

This leads to a spirited debate of fun first day of school activities and we finally convince Cohen to try a game instead of a full explanation of the syllabus that students will never remember by the second day. Cohen leaves the room and I can still hear the squeak of his shoes on the floor as Jade shuts the door and springs into action.

"He barely looked at me the entire meeting. And I thought my hair looked pretty good today," she laments while fluffing her red wavy locks, never breaking eye contact.

"I was leading the meeting, so I'm sure that's why he even looked at me. And your bangs look incredible today. Did you try something new?" I question, trying to distract her with her favorite subject.

Unconvinced, she smirks. "I will tell you all about it when we get home, but don't even try it. You two have chemistry. That's all I'm saying."

"He's my mentee Jade," I chide.

"So? There aren't any rules about dating your mentee. And you guys are practically the same age, so you can't use that one either. You're just being stubborn and you know it."

I glance down at my watch. "Oh crap, we really are going to be late for the craft session," I point out.

With a groan, Jade says, "Go ahead without me. I don't care if I'm fashionably late to arts and crafts."

With that, I'm off to waste time that I could be working in my classroom.

Chapter Four

Elle

I 'm silently questioning my life choices and all career aspirations as I squint, trying to decipher the directions and pieces littered on the table. It's looking more like an I Spy scene, than a completed birdhouse at the moment. Adding to the visual clutter, there are bags of beads and gems that would look more at home in a kindergarten prize box. Apparently, birds care about aesthetics now? I could spend time thinking about all the ways this is a waste of time or doesn't make sense, but that seems like a lot of mental energy for another one of the random things our admin does.

Reminiscent of high school cliques, the English department sits together at one table. Then, the math, science, and history teachers are in their sections. The coaches hang together at another table, separate from their subjects. Leaving us, the CTE group, on the other side. I'm flanked by Cohen and Jade, who are staring at the directions with the same bewilderment. This doesn't bode well for our birdhouse.

My thoughts are interrupted by the crackling of feedback from the microphone, as assistant principal Ezra addresses us.

"You've had a long day of working in your classrooms, so as a reward, what says teambuilding like arts and crafts?" He lets out a laugh as if he actually believes what he's saying.

Jade elbows me and nods to the table. I glance down and have to practice a yoga breath not to burst out laughing. She's spelled HELP with the beads. Cohen glances down when he notices us not paying attention and can't hold back his laugh. All heads turn in our direction, forcing Jade and I to quickly wipe away the bead message before anyone can notice.

"See, Cohen gets it already!" Ezra says, tone deaf as usual. "You've got to have fun too. What's life without a little whimsy now and then?"

Jade whispers, "Whimsy? What is he on?" I elbow her hard to shut her up and nod toward Cohen. We can't diminish every activity and dull his new teacher sparkle, it should dull naturally over the course of the year like the rest of us. Jade and I enter a silent stare down, in which she finally sighs dramatically and pastes on a fake smile complete with an eye roll.

We can't afford for Cohen to want to quit before classes even start. It's difficult to find teachers who are experts in a subject matter like this, so when there's a new CTE teacher, fanfare is always involved. He'll be the shiny new golden child for a while.

Left to our own devices, we divide and conquer, taking different sections to assemble. Since they couldn't provide us with a simple structure, the three of us have to share a semi elaborate model.

We're chatting and laughing. Jade's explaining the high school ecosystem to Cohen and I don't register her plan when she adds, "Hey, Elle. Will you hold down that side piece for me?"

I do it without hesitation, placing a hand on the birdhouse, only to realize this puts me directly in Cohen's space. His eyes widen a bit, and I glare at Jade who is biting her lip, trying to hide a smile. Both of us are unable to move until the glue dries and we look like we're playing a game of Twister.

Our arms are touching, and our pinkies are dangerously close. I can feel the warmth from his body heat through his sleeve and it's making my skin crawl.

I should not be this close to my mentee. I can smell the faint clean scent of his body wash. It seems like something that would have a name like ocean breeze. I nonchalantly take another whiff and then stop myself. It starts by being this close, then it graduates to other things that I'm not even entertaining. Moral of the story is I should not know what my mentee smells like.

Determined to take the attention off my proximity to Cohen, I attempt to make conversation. With Jade. "What color do we think Angela dyed her hair over the summer?"

Jade squints in concentration. "Hmmm, she was going through a school spirit phase once she became debate captain, so my guess is green."

Riley the law enforcement teacher, who finished his birdhouse a while ago, jumps in. "That would be a look. Maybe gold? That is the more natural option of our school colors."

I step in. "Exactly, which is why it'll be green. Remember when we were all talking in the hallway and Riley jumped when he saw the rainbow?"

Riley justifies, "I just wasn't expecting it. I had gotten used to the pink. She told me she does it all herself. That takes some serious skill."

"And I heard Andy hit a growth spurt, so Riley be prepared, he just may be taller than you now," Jade says with a smile.

"Awww I'm going to miss having someone shorter than me. There's always hope for the freshmen, though?" I tease.

Everyone laughs at my comment as we continue to work on our crafts.

Feeling guilty for talking about students Cohen hadn't had yet, I make an effort to include him. "We are all in the same hallway, so we see the same group of kids and get to know them. You'll be able to join in once school starts."

With a smile, Cohen answers, "It sounds like I got the best hallway."

"We are simultaneously the loudest hallway and the most fun," Riley chimes in, while delicately dabbing a piece of exposed glue on the end of our bird house.

"Why loud?" Cohen asks.

"His groups are running drills. If you hear, PUT YOUR HANDS UP, or STOP RESISTING, they're just practice scenarios," I explain.

Riley laughs and looks at me. "Don't act like your kids are silent. Those film nerds are dressing up, acting out scenes, and generally always trying to stick a camera in your face in the hallway."

"Well, that's why I have students currently in —""Film school," Jade and Riley say in sync with me.

Herald walks over to join our group with a huff. "I could be on my couch right now, but nope, I just made a birdhouse someone else is going to take home," he laments.

Herald is two years away from retirement. You don't have to ask me how I know, he'll tell you at least once a day. I wouldn't be surprised if he has a countdown clock as his screensaver. I'm sure I would be burnt out too, but a familiar pang of guilt riles in my stomach. I take back any pessimistic thoughts. While everyone goes in ebbs and flows of burnout, I could only hope someone would rip away my badge if I ever match the level of this guy. He can't see the flowers, since he's too busy dissecting the weeds.

I'm nervous to even have Cohen around him. I don't want any of the jaded attitude to rub off on him. Do I already feel protective of him because he's my mentee, or something else? No, definitely just because he's my mentee.

Trying to add some spunk, I weakly add, "Well at least we're not going over testing procedure."

"I'm sure that's tomorrow's plan," Herald mumbles.

Giving up, I turn my focus to the slightly lopsided birdhouse. I swear we followed the directions to the T. Maybe it's just the angle. I turn my head, trying to decide.

"It's crooked," Cohen confirms dejectedly.

We work on fixing the birdhouse until we're dismissed for the day.

Right as we all strap on our bags and grab the cups littering the cafeteria, Ezra the AP calls out to the room, "One more thing..." My eyes shoot up as I'm almost antsy with worry at what that phrase will add to my plate.

He finishes in a mock cheery tone. "We need chaperones for the Back 2 Cool event, so check the sheets by the door to see your predetermined roles." A chorus of groans meet his statement.

On top of the last-minute notice about staying late, predetermined roles were the worst. You couldn't pick a spot near friends to make the time pass any faster. Trying not to look too annoyed at this statement for Cohen, I tried to smile at him as we walked almost shoulder to shoulder with the group to see what we had.

Chapter Five

Cohen

The next morning, I laugh to myself as I pack my lunch replaying Elle's reaction when she realized she got the job of food inspector. "What even is that?" she muttered under her breath before trying to mask her true feelings with a wide smile. No one was actually that positive about duty with a made-up title. Luckily for me, the first-year teachers got to ease into duty, helping anywhere we want.

I set my mind back on the task ahead as I realized I forgot to get groceries. Again. Rustling in the pantry to scavenge something must have been louder than I thought, because my roommate trudges into view, looking half asleep.

"Cohen, seriously? What are you doing?" Ren answers.

Ren and I met in college during a freshman-year group project. When we both ended up in the same town postgrad, we decided to get an apartment together. He's a business exec—I can never remember the details of what he actually does, and makes a bunch of money doing it. He's really just doing me a favor because he knows I can't afford to live by myself on my teaching salary alone. I don't want to think about the day he and his girlfriend decide to move in together and I have to figure something else out.

"Sorry, I'm trying to find a five-course meal in the desert. There could be tumbleweeds in here. We need to go grocery shopping," I complain, sighing at the pantry in defeat.

"You need to go grocery shopping. Take some of my food if it will get you to stop. Remember, just because you get up early to play teacher, doesn't mean I have to." With that, he turns and stumbles back to his room, closing the door with a slam. Did I mention he has several redeeming qualities? Logical, fair, loyal, organized - but being a morning person doesn't make the cut.

With a shrug, I grab one of his pre-portioned meals from the fridge and run out the door before he can change his mind. This is way better than the can of olives and bag of chips I was planning.

I have a few minutes before I have to leave, so when my phone rings, and I see my mom's name on the screen, I answer with a sigh.

"Cohen, you actually answered this time," she chirps. She's usually not this passive aggressive, but I haven't talked to her in a week and missed the last family dinner.

"Mom, you know I've been busy with school stuff," I say, cringing at my lame excuse.

"Son, your brothers and sister miss you. And your father and I will forget what you look like if we don't see you soon. Family dinner is this week and would be the perfect way to make it up to us."

It's not that I don't want to see my family, but they hound me on my ten-year plan and it stresses me out. Do I have a girlfriend? Do I not want a girlfriend? Why can't I get a girlfriend?

"Mom, I'm trying, but I probably won't be at family dinner until school starts. Our days run long and I have to stay late to get extra help from Elle, my mentor," I explain, pacing.

Her voice perks up. "Elle, that's a cute name. Is she single?"

"I don't know, Mom, I haven't asked her."

"Well, maybe you should. You know what? Don't let us get in the way of your time with your mentor. Family dinners will still be there once school starts.""Thanks, Mom." I cringe. Even though I found a way out of this for now, I have a feeling this will come back on me later.

We hang up, and I try to push my mom's words from my head. As I make my way out the door with the fifty bags I have to carry painfully crashing into my legs with each stride, I try to take a deep breath to ease the pit in my stomach. Normally, I can walk into any situation and fake my way through until I actually know what I'm doing. So far, teaching hasn't been that way, and I'm wondering if it's me or the job. Instead of focusing on that, I look at the lush green trees Arkansans typically take for granted.

I can practically envision myself hiking up a hill in Devil's Den, shaded by the dense treeline. That vision is quickly interrupted by the stack of papers I have to grade and lesson plans that need to be done for the next week. I guess the closest I'll get to the outdoors is the nature ambience on my computer screen.

Sometimes, all you can do is nod. I would like to consider myself resourceful, an expert Googler if you will, but lately, when someone is telling me something teaching related, I don't even know what questions to ask or what to research later to decode our conversation.

And everyone keeps giving me that knowing look or smile and saying something to the equivalent of," You don't know what you don't know,"

or,

"All teachers don't know what they're doing their first year."

But how am I ever supposed to learn what to do when everyone talks in acronyms, and never actually explains anything. Take this email I just got from admin. It makes my head spin just reading all the teaching terms crammed in.

I sigh and close my laptop as I hang my head in defeat and drag myself to my mentor's classroom for the millionth time that day. I want to stop myself from seeming like an incompetent idiot, asking her lengthy questions after every email, but it looks like that day won't be today. I have tried talking to the other new teachers, but we all just pour over every word trying to decipher the jargon in front of us, furrowing our brows in concentration, as if we are trying to adjust the matrix.

I will give it to Elle, she hasn't given up on me like some of the other first year's mentors. And after the impression I've left after completely freaking her out with my flirting and a conversation full of innuendos I would rather not remember, I can't figure out how I can get her to see me as more than a mentee.

I know it may not be encouraged, but there's no rule against dating a co-worker/mentor, and every time I look into her eyes, I can't help but wonder if it would ever happen. But it's only day two, so maybe that conversation with my mom got to me more than I thought.

As I trudge into Elle's classroom, I lift my head to see another first year already there. She is sitting at her desk typing out something while laughing at whatever he said. He sits in one of the student desks with his laptop up and I can see his smirk from here. If I remember correctly, his mentor is right across the hall, so he should defer to them instead of monopolizing her time.

She glances up and smiles. "Hey, I was just about to get you. Are you here to ask about the letter admin sent out?"

I nod in response.

Elle instantly goes into teacher mode. "So, I'm going to decode this email for you guys, but just know, it doesn't actually matter and it's just another hoop we have to jump through. Admin have too many fires to put out, and can't possibly check on every teachers' learning objectives every day. In reality, I would suggest only updating learning objectives on your board when you switch units, or honestly every time admin observes, so they won't see the same thing twice."

My shoulders instantly relax as I breathe a sigh of relief. Elle makes everything seem doable. It's easy to catastrophize every little thing as a new teacher. As if your classroom can be ripped from your grasp the moment you don't submit a lesson plan on time or have a check mark in the needs improvement column of your evaluations.

Now that I've thought about it, I have to knock on wood. The phrase 'needs improvement' is the teaching equivalent of shouting Macbeth backstage right before curtain to a group full of superstitious theater students; you just don't do it.

I shake the thoughts out of my head with what I pass off as a head nod, as Elle continues, and I need to listen to her instead of spiraling further. I've decided to fixate on the curl sitting on her shoulder. It bounces with every animated movement. She's in her element, and I can't help but feel a pang of jealousy. Will I ever feel this confident?

"And that's all you need to know," she finishes.

Welp, so much for listening to her. The other first year thanks her and starts to leave, but I stay put. She told me earlier that her classroom was always open, so I want to take full advantage. For educational purposes of course.

Deciding to just go for it, my words tumble out before I can chicken out of asking. "I need help with something and I'm totally out of my depth." This should be my new catchphrase at this point.

Elle nods encouragingly. "Sure, what is it?"

I wince in embarrassment. "So... I kind of suck at putting together my bulletin boards. I mean what's even supposed to be on them anyway?"

Her eyes light up as if lunch duty was cancelled for the year. "Well, first you have to have the right materials. And we'll figure out the rest together." She was smiling and I had to snap myself out of it before I got completely sidetracked.

I caught myself staring and before the moment got awkward, I ask, "Where do I find the materials?"

"I have some you can borrow, but what's your theme?" she questions, slowly walking back to what she affectionately refers to as the crap closet.

"Theme?" I clarify. Was this another assignment I was unaware of?

"Yeah, your classroom theme or color scheme? I want to match it to your bulletin boards if they're going to be hanging in your room all year." She purses her lips in anticipation of what I'm assuming is supposed to be a well thought out answer.

"Can my theme be high school? Or is that too bleak? And my color scheme could be the colors the room is now. Well, in addition to my Die Hard movie posters. The design on them is surprisingly well done. Speaking of Die Hard, what's your stance on the legitimacy of it as a Christmas film?" I probe eagerly. Who knew I could make bulletin boards fun.

She stares at me with a slightly open mouth and narrowed eyes, as if I had suggested my color scheme was puke green with a side of poop brown for good measure. "First off, it takes place during a Christmas party, so it's obviously a Christmas movie."

Point one in favor of Elle. She locked in her spot as my favorite teacher at the school.

"You're really not going to pick a color scheme? Your room is bland and depressing right now." She looks at me expectantly.

"Of course it is," I counter. "I haven't added the posters yet." I almost add a duh to the end of that sentence but think better of it.

Elle looks up to the ceiling for a moment, summoning her patience interacting with me. "Let me think on it, and I'll get back to you." She suggests all the earlier excitement erased from her features.

CHAPTER SIX

Elle

The characteristically sharp smell of stale school lunch fills my nostrils as I step into the cafeteria. Luckily for all in attendance, the event is a potluck, and members of the PTA will bring food that is pointedly more edible. While food inspector has to be the most made-up title I'd ever heard of and code for we just need more chaperones, aka warm bodies at this event, I count myself lucky to have such a simple job. All I have to do is serve the food and make sure everything is clean and refilled.

I share a look of solidarity with Jade from across the room who has one of the worst jobs of the event, ticket collector. Being at the front and having to monitor everyone coming and going is a thankless task. What is that saying? Adults make the worst students. Parents shove each other and impatiently sigh at their phones as they wait in what is more of a zig zag than a straight line. I can hear the raised voice of a parent piercing the air, stabbing their finger at their ticket. Jade's face remains calm, but I can tell she is actively trying not to roll her eyes.

"I bought my ticket three weeks ago, check the list again." The parent screeches in a voice so high pitched, it could break glass.

Boldly, I watch Jade give her the finger, holding up her pointer finger that is, to indicate she will be a minute as she checks with the student council chair. Now there's someone who doesn't make enough to match the non-stop fun that is student council and all the scrutiny that comes with it.

In the five seconds Jade is away from her post, I catch the parents exchanging conspiratorial glances, and one of them makes a move as if to slip into the event without a ticket. I power walk over to the station with a speed any granny would envy and stand in front of the parents with a smile. They sigh in indignation and slip back into line, making the zig zag formation, zag a bit more.

Back with reinforcements, Jade nods for me to head back to my post, and I hurry to get away from that drama as soon as possible.

As I trudge back to the exciting job of food inspector, I notice movement out of the corner of my eye. There is Cohen, pen in hand, signing one paper and moving to the next, taking a thoughtful second to read, hovering his pen above another sheet, ready to sign his free time away.

With abject terror I realize he is signing up for multiple committees. The PTA capitalizes on an event with parents and teacher in one place, and has an entire table available of committees to volunteer for. There's everything from the Prom to scholarship committees.

No, no, no. I'm struck by the sudden déjà vu of a first-year teacher version of myself, making the exact same mistake. Only, I know how that turned out for me, and I have to stop him from repeating my idealistic rookie mistakes.

In a desperate panic, I race over and snatch the clipboard out of his hands. Normally I would be more delicate, but he's not using an erasable writing utensil. Drastic measures must be taken.

He looks up at me in confusion, as I practically shout at him, "How many?"

"How many, what?" he asks.

"How many committees have you signed up for? We might be able to fix this with some carefully placed white out..."

Switching his weight from one foot to the other, he questions, "Why would I not want to sign up for committees? I don't know many teachers or parents at this school, and it's a way to meet people not in my hallway."

I take a breath to steady my voice. "That's a fantastic point. I would pick a max of two committees for that exact purpose. If you do more than that, all your weeknights after school will be filled. You're gonna need that time for planning, grading, and having a life with what's left of your free time. Just trust me," I plead.

He doesn't break eye contact as he slowly lowers his pen, taking the clipboard from me and putting it back on the table. With wide eyes, he confesses, "So, I may have already signed up for five."

"Stay here, and I'll get my white out," I say as I walk in the direction of my room. As if he didn't hear me, Cohen is on my heels.

Once that crisis is averted, I make my way back to my post at the food table and I notice a student lingering a bit too long without grabbing anything to eat. Please say he just wanted to survey the options and didn't put contact solution in the punch or something. The last thing I need is an entire group of parents with food poisoning. I would never hear the end of it.

I'm at my post without incident and trying not to fall asleep standing up. I can hear the Muppet sounding muffled microphone voice echoing from the crackly speakers in the auditorium as the assistant principals finish up the parent presentation.

The parent of one of my former student's friends walks up to the food table and I smile, grateful for the company. That may sound like a weird thing, but in CTE classes, kids stay with us for four years, and since we all bus to contests together and our classrooms are close together, we know more than our selected students. Oftentimes, we even get to know our students' friends, who come with them to our rooms like Michael, and become extra members of the group. I call them the video groupies in my head.

"Hey, Mrs. Dannon, how are you? Michael still talks about the game with the buzzers you let him join in at lunch. He wishes his teachers this year used them."

"Hey, Mr. Anders. He can always bring his own buzzers to class. I'm sure his teacher would love that," I respond. I don't bother to tell him it's actually Miss Dannon, because it's such a common mistake I barely notice anymore.

He chuckles. "I'm sure she would. It was great to run into you."

As he walks away, I'm already lost in my own thoughts, brainstorming how I can incorporate the buzzers next year. I hear a noise so slight I have to crane my ears to hear, realizing it's coming in Mr. Anders' direction. I jump with a start as I watch him clutch his stomach and slide down to the floor face-first.

No one in their right mind would lay down on those floors face-first, so I know the pain must be all consuming. I rush over, surprised he was able to gain that much ground in the minute or two since we spoke. He makes continued gurgling sounds that remind me of an engine desperately trying to sputter to life. Numb with fear, I start doing the only logical thing I think of.

I rise to decibels I didn't know I was capable of as I scream, "Help! Nurse, Mr. Anders needs help." My screams mix with the chorus of parent voices in a morbid tune as the assembly releases and they start to file in. Gasps accompany the hammering of footsteps as I can only hope a doctor or the school nurse are on their way. Luckily, a parent who is a doctor shoves me out the way and checks for a pulse and then starts doing chest compressions.

He tries to ask me questions to take a guess at what happened, but I'm not much help. I feel numb. I was just talking to him a few minutes ago, and now he's lying there, unmoving.

"What happened? Did you see him go down?" He fires off.

"Yes. He uh, stopped at the," I take a big gulp, fighting tears, "food table, and uh walked away. Then a minute later he held his stomach and collapsed."

"Did he eat anything?" the parent demands.

"I think so." I try to rack my brain and it comes up with a hazy image of Mr. Anders with fork in hand.

Time drags on in a mind-numbing blur as waves of nausea and dizziness wash over me. Then, cutting sharply through the haze of shock, I find myself face to face with Riley, the law enforcement teacher. I can't look him in the eye, hypnotized by the badge around his neck. He wasn't wearing that while teaching.

He clears his throat, and I jump. "Ms. Dannon, you witnessed Mr. Ander's fall?"

Wait. I knew that he was still a detective and sometimes helped the department, but this looked really official. And why wasn't he calling me by my first name?

Trying to piece everything together, I stumble over my words. "Yes, it was me—uh—it was me that saw him fall," I stutter, not elaborating.

With a voice that I could only assume he used to talk to those who still need nap time, he asks, "Can you tell me about it?"

I recount the story in hazy detail, doing the best I can muster, but my brain only registers every third word. "Talk" "Anders" "Stomach" "Falling" "Gurgle." After what feels like an eternity stumbling through Riley's questions, I am emotionally drained. I feel like a bottle of glue on the last day of school. Misshapen, past its prime, and missing a cap. I almost run into the food table, which makes my stomach churn at the thought. Did someone do something to the food while I was grabbing white-out?

I shake my head to push the thoughts away. I have no idea what happened, it could be totally unrelated to the food. Even though it's illogical, this somehow feels like I did something wrong. Maybe if I would've been at the table the whole time, this wouldn't have happened.

The odor of a cacophony of different dishes that don't go together fill my nostrils as they sit and rot, ready to be bagged in evidence. I instinctively know like any good armchair detective, that they'll have to bag everything to test. Shouldn't there be crime scene tape around this thing? It hits me, Mr. Anders is gluten free. The PTA moms feel sorry for him and always make him a special dish, and to my knowledge, he's the only one that ever eats it. With the sudden bounce of an excited puppy, I bound back over to the detective.

The strain of today is evident in the breaths I take as my hands go straight to my thighs to catch my breath. To save my dignity, I don't drop them fully to my knees. I really do need to get on an exercise regime.

"I—" sucking in air, "remembered"—cough—"something," I practically shout.

Riley has his back to me, so I shouted all that to his shoulder blades. He slowly turns around and looks at me as if I have donned a magnifying glass and Sherlock Holmes hat and told him I can solve the crime.

"Ok." He frowns. "What did you remember?"

His lack of enthusiasm at case cracking information is alarming, but I persist. "Mr. Anders is gluten free. He gets a specialized dish made for him at every event." I suck in a dramatic breath as I piece together."Meaning he was the target! Whoever poisoned him knew what dish to add it to!"

Parents in the vicinity gasp and start whispering to each other. Jessie's dad, the one that has a family YouTube channel, holds a phone up, the bright white light indicating he isn't going to miss the chance to go viral.

Riley's head whips back and forth with the ferocity of a student hyped up on sugar. I worry that he may need to see a chiropractor after this if his neck doesn't snap right then.

"Why are you so intent on making my life miserable? We don't know anything yet," he snaps.

Confused by his knee jerk reaction. Making his life miserable? We don't even talk that often. He must be stressed if witnessing a crime has somehow put me on his list. "I'm helping you with the investigation, detective..." I pause mid-sentence, "teacher, what is your official title?"

"It's detective Riley for now. Since I was a detective with the LAPD, and the department is short staffed, I'm helping on a case-by-case basis. And remembering random facts may help in some small way, but an actual investigation takes extensive research and checking of those facts." He scoffs. "That's why we don't announce them. Out loud. For freaked out parents with cell phones within earshot."

My cheeks turn pink, berating myself about my rookie mistake. I feel like this isn't the time to remind him that I solved the case of the missing SD cards all by myself while wrangling a class of hooligans, but I feel like the subtleties of my skills will be lost on him. He's all business right now. Not the teacher I chat with between classes.

I'm at a loss. Anytime I talk to Riley in the hall, he's always nice. I mean, formal and cordial, but never this agitated. It feels like I'm missing something, but clearly this isn't the weirdest thing to happen to me today. Getting the sense that my information isn't of value to him, I decide to drop it until I can catch my breath and hopefully think of something that will actually help. I just can't get the image of the body bag, I mean Mr. Anders, being rolled away. It happened during Riley's questioning, and I could only focus on that while he spoke.

Just thinking of the news that's coming his son's way makes my stomach twist. No one should be without their dad because I couldn't man a food table. I somehow screwed up being a food inspector. The title that seemed made up, didn't seem so fake anymore.

I can tell by the squinty glare being torpedoed my way, that detective Riley would very much like to get away from this conversation. His fists clench briefly, then, catching me looking down, he slowly uncurls them and lets his hands rest flat against his thighs. I turn to leave without a word, hoping by some miracle I can go home and not toss and turn all night, plagued with thoughts of this evening's events.

Before I get far, I hear heavy footsteps behind me. Riley barks, "Elle, stop." I turn around to find him glaring at me. "I didn't release you."

"Oh," is all that comes out of my mouth meekly. We both stare at each other for another beat.

"What else did you need to ask me?" I ask warily.

"Nothing," Riley confirms. He reaches into his pocket, and pulls out a card. "Call me if you remember anything else." As if I can't just call him on his classroom phone. Once he places the card in my palm, he concedes, "Now, you're dismissed."

He starts to walk away, and I shout at his back, "If I have any information, I can just walk next door to your room." He doesn't say anything, but gives me a curt wave, never turning back to me.

A weird power play to end the worst day in existence. How am I going to ease the guilt churning in my stomach? What if this case never gets solved? Can I live with that?

CHAPTER SEVEN

Cohen

On the first day of school I stride into Elle's room only to stop short, almost tripping over the carpet. I feel like I'm interrupting something. She's hunched over her computer, intently staring at her screen. She's so entranced, she hasn't noticed me yet. I walk over and fling the papers in my hands on her desk, and they land directly on top of her hands over the keyboard.

She jumps slightly as if I snuck up on her and says, "Oh hey, you're here early."

As she tries to shut her laptop when I round the corner of her desk, I catch the laptop first. "Whatcha doin?"

"Just getting my first day of school slides done," she sing-songs. No one is that cheery about slide decks.

"Sure, I would believe you, but Elle Dannon doesn't get things ready for the first day of school the day of," I reason.

"Spill it or I'll take your mail back to your box," I challenge, holding out the stack of mail from her box.

"Wait, you got my mail?" She meets my eyes for the first time. She looks as if I bought her a bouquet of flowers.

"Yeah, I was already there," I mutter, trying to remain cool. Just being the nice mentee, sucking up to his mentor. Totally normal.

"Stop trying to change the subject. What are you doing, Elle?"

She looks back down at her laptop not wanting to meet my eyes. She speaks so fast, it takes my brain a second to catch up. "I was feeling bad about Mr. Anders, since it was my fault I was away from my post, and Riley won't take me seriously, but I want to find out who did this to Mr. Anders. So I'm going to do it."

"Do what?"

"Solve the case," she concludes, with a look of pure determination.

"The case? Elle, you're not Veronica Mars. You can't go around righting wrongs. We're teachers, not detectives. We use a Smartboard, not a murder board," I reason.

I snap my fingers as I realize what she's hiding. "Wait, are you working on your murder board?"

"I mean..." She trails off while slowly closing her laptop with a strained smile.

Laughing, I close the gap and swat her hand away, so I can open her laptop, and yep. It's a murder board. The most organized murder board I've ever seen.

"Elle?"

"Yep."

"Did you actually create an entire digital murder board?" I say, trying to get the words out without laughing but fail miserably.

"Just go away, Cohen. You can laugh because you're not the reason someone is dead," she huffs. Her eyes turn glassy, and she sniffs while crossing her arms.

Realizing she doesn't understand I'm laughing at the situation, not her, I swoop down to her level and put my hands on her arms to steady her before I have time to think about my actions.

"You're not any more to blame for his death than me for taking you away from the table."

A beat of silence passes, and her eyes tell me, she's already reached the same conclusion.

"Elle?" I say, hoping she'll be receptive.

"Yep."

"Let's solve this together." Determination fills my body. If she's gonna put herself in danger, I'm going to be right there with her.

"Cohen, I think it's best if I do this solo." She scoffs.

I figure that reasoning with her is the only way to get through. "You're about as subtle as a car bomb. If you start asking questions, people will figure you out in five seconds. But, I'm a new teacher. It's practically my job to ask questions. And I can charm my way through our investigation and no one will suspect a thing."

"You just had to call yourself charming, didn't you? What skills do you have that would help with the investigation? Besides your charm?" She makes air quotes on charm. She's just getting me back, so I'm choosing to not get offended.

She takes my silence as an opportunity to shake her shoulders, freeing herself from my grasp and forcing me to step back to the outer perimeter of her desk.

I pretend to mule it over. By the jut of her jaw, I can tell if I make a joke out of this she's shutting her laptop and requesting a new mentee.

She turns her gaze back to her laptop to continue working on the board. When she hears me start to speak she looks up.

I take a deep breath as I start, barely able to believe I'm about to be vulnerable in an attempt to win her trust. "Ok, fine. I'm good at blending in."

She huffs out a laugh in disbelief.

"Hear me out. I'm the youngest child of four, and I was so unnoticeable, my family left me at a gas station on our trip to Florida. The cashier had to call my parents number and tell them I wasn't in the car. They didn't even realize it." With a resigned sigh, I continue, "It's gotten better as I got older, and now we're so close you wouldn't know it, but it wasn't always the way it is now."

Her features soften as her face shifts into listening mode, realizing I'm serious this time. Then, noticing she's not scowling anymore, she quickly tries to settle her expression back into something neutral.

"I have always been invisible to my family, they're loud enough that I just let them lead," I blurt, before I can put too much thought into what I'm oversharing.

Elle finishes for me, "So you overcompensate by always seeming calm and collected as a coping mechanism to make everyone feel like nothing bothers you even when it does?"

My eyes widen in shock as I struggle to right myself in this conversation. That got real, real fast.

"Some of that may be trueish, but I don't think that shaped my entire personality."

"Our past experiences are the puzzle pieces of our adult psyche. I bet it affects you more than you think even though clearly, you're not ready to fully admit it. You'll see it with your students. And as you get to know their siblings and parents and find out more about their backstory, you'll notice the patterns. Just wait and see."

How do I always find myself spilling my guts to her? I go in thinking we're having a conversation about school and end up telling her my entire backstory. Trying to figure out how I just got psychoanalyzed before 7:00 a.m., I shake my head in an effort to get myself back on track.

"Anyway, I'm your best secret weapon because I can blend in when we're doing recon but put on the charm for fact finding missions. I come across more chill and less noticeable which would work in your favor."

"Recon? We're not in an episode of Blue Bloods, this is an actual case. And if Riley figures out what we're doing, it could have real consequences."

"Which is exactly why you need me, you need someone on your team, Elle. You can't color code your way through this case. You need help. All the best crime fighters were teams."

"I'm pretty sure Nancy Drew worked alone," she fires back.

"Scooby and the GANG? Or Shawn Spencer AND Gus. Even Beckett needed Castle, Benson needed Stabler, I could go on and on."

"Agree to disagree about Benson needing Stabler, but I see your point. It has been frustrating trying to do it all on my own," she admits.

She throws her head back in surrender. I think. Or frustration?

"Ok, fine, I'll give you a chance."

At my smile, she clarifies, "But if you get in my way, you're off MY case. Got it?"

I nod, not wanting to screw this up with the wrong answer.

She sighs in resignation. "I'll share the murder board with you. Meet me after school for a mentor meeting so I can catch you up."

"Well, happy first day of school, E." Before she can object or change her mind, I race out of her room and start running through what I have to set up for class today.

At least with all this murder business, I haven't had time to think about how I'm about to get a crash course in teaching. Buckle up.

I've aged five years and it's only 9:30 a.m. It's not as if I thought teaching would be easy, but this is brutal.

"You look like you've been through battle and lost." Elle giggles, as she joins me out in the hall.

"Maybe you should just quit now," she suggests with a smile.

"I wouldn't want to end your mentoring reign so soon. I'll stay for now. If I make it through the day," I say as we both start laughing.

A few students give us the side eye as they look up from their schedules to locate their room number. One student sneers at us as he makes his way into, of course, my classroom. He's going to be fun, I can just tell.

She steps closer to me and lowers her voice. "I was thinking about our project. We should work on it outside of school grounds."

I smirk. "Elle, if you want to go on a date, all you had to do was ask." Dang it. Why do I always default to flirting? But she really gave me no choice with that set up.

She looks affronted, as if I took her flair pens away. Ouch. "First, if you're not going to take this seriously, I'll do it by myself."

I sigh, "I didn't mean it, I'll—"

She cuts me off. "And second, don't say things like that in the hallway. Students will overhear and we'll never hear the end of it."

Still not seeing the downside of that, I nod, all possible comebacks vanished. Getting rejected was not on my bingo card for the day, but based on the way it has been going, it doesn't seem far off. Does it really count if I wasn't serious?

Out of the corner of my eye I see another person walk up. It's Riley, the law enforcement teacher.

"How's life in gen pop?" he questions.

Elle seems unfazed by the comment, though she's twisting her hands nervously. Is she uncomfortable or nervous around him? I feel like there's a backstory there I'm not privy to. I'll have to file that away for later. I swear I've seen them laughing in the hallway before.

"I still miss our building, but it hasn't been too bad for me. I have some sweethearts," she finishes, smiling to herself. I remember someone telling me they had a building just for the CTE kids before they got too big, and we all got plopped in the middle of the school.

"What about you, newbie, do you have any sweethearts?" He smirks as if he's amusing himself. Amateur.

I wasn't sure how to answer the question truthfully. I just met my first group of students five minutes ago and I did most of the talking, so other than glazed eyes staring back at me, I don't have much of an impression yet.

When in doubt, double down. I dawn my best southern belle accent and drawl, "Bless my heart, I just have the most thoughtful group."

Returning back to my normal register, I finish, "I already found gum under the computer tables and confiscated a phone, so we're off to a solid start."

"Mssssss Danonnnnn." Pierces through the air as a group of girls run up to Elle and envelop her in hugs.

"Hey, I missed you! How was your summer?" Her megawatt smile is on full display. Will she ever smile at me that way? I shake myself out of my trance, trying to look cool, and I notice Riley smirking at me. Clearly, he misses nothing. I'll have to keep that in mind.

"Oooh just wait until I tell you about my trip to the Bahamas. I filmed a vlog that I can email you," the student says in an excited high-pitched tone.

"Yes, I'd love to see it!" Elle trills as they walk into her classroom.

"They seem fun," I say, jealous of her ease with them. She seems so at ease with the whole teaching thing. It's hard not to be jealous.

Elle's eyes are shining as she glances at me. "They are. Just wait until you have students for multiple years. It's the best feeling to see your favorites back again."

"I thought we weren't supposed to have favorites? Teachers love all their students equally and all that," I say with my hand over my heart in mock surprise.

Elle and Riley give me knowing looks and laugh. I notice the change in their expression, as they spot someone down the hall. I turn to look and find a teacher smiling and waving in our direction. I shoot her a halfhearted smile before turning back to them.

"Ok, what's the deal with her?" I ask, hoping to get a primer before she makes her way over.

Elle whispers out of the side of her mouth, "That's Layla. She's a total kiss-up and drives us all crazy. She keeps trying to sit with us at lunch, and we always find an excuse."

Riley scoffs. "Seriously, avoid her if you can. I used to let her borrow my dry erase markers, and we conveniently had the same duty every event the rest of the year. I swear she switched spots with other teachers."

Elle panics. "Quick, she's almost here, disperse."

They wave in her direction and beeline for their classrooms just as the bell sounds.

Chapter Eight

Elle

There are some things that you can't teach. Yes, I know that sounds harsh coming from a teacher, but every once in a while you have to learn through experiences, and you can lecture someone all day, but until they go through it, they just won't know. Case in point at lunch today.

I dramatically slam my pb&j down, as five pairs of eyes stare back at me.

"That bad, huh?" Brittany, the Marketing teacher sympathizes.

"So it all started in fourth period." A chorus of groans interrupts my thought.

"They should ban classes before lunch," another teacher chimes in.

"Or kids should suck it up, we're all tired and hungry," Herald laments.

Someone please enter this man in Publisher's Clearing House so he has an excuse to leave the classroom.

Just as our conversation is gaining momentum, Jade walks in. "When will this school ever give us tissues? If I have to steal one more roll of toilet paper from the bathroom..."

"Stop complaining, you're using the fancy tissues, I've been using the paper towel roll since the start of school. I've already had to send three kids to the nurse for nose bleeds," Herald complains.

Cohen's voice chimes in, "I buy tissues for my classroom." All heads in the room are on a sharp swivel towards his voice.

"You have tissue money? How much are new teachers paid now? Wait, I don't want to know, it's too depressing," Herald laments.

Cohen continues, "Tissues are a basic human right and practically on Maslow's Hierarchy of Needs and I prioritize buying tissues with my own money, so my students can have a quality learning experience. And not get bodily fluids on my computers."

One small chuckle turns into a chorus of laughter as every other teacher in the room bursts into hysterics. Me included.

"Tell me that tomorrow when you've gone through all your tissues," Jade says under her breath just loud enough for him to hear.

Layla chooses that exact moment to walk by lunch box in hand. "Hey guys, can I join you for lunch?"

Herald balls up a food wrapper. "Actually, this is a lunch meeting."

Brittany chimes in, "Yeah, CTE teachers only, sorry."

Layla's forlorn expression makes me want to cut through the group's lies and just let her sit with us. But then I remember how she tried to become a trio with Jade and I and wouldn't leave us alone. We had to start taking another path away from her classroom and she eventually forgot about us.

"Ok, have a good lunch," she meekly replies before walking back down the hallway.

Not the only one in the room feeling guilty, Jade asks, "Are we being too mean?"

"No. Even her own department can't stand her. She crashed their group lunches last year and I heard they all eat alone in their classrooms now," Brittany says.

"I have to put up with student chaos all day, and I just need a relaxing lunch. Maybe she'll find her group in the first years? They seem eager to please." Everyone nods and goes back to eating their lunch, trying to forget about Layla.

The next day Brittany, the Marketing teacher, is at the white board, dry erase marker in one hand and a sandwich in the other. She's the school gossip and always roams the hallway talking to teachers, eager to show off her skills.

Stepping back from her latest creation, we all take in the rudimentary murder board she's concocted from everything she's heard so far, when a haggard Cohen walks in before we have time to discuss it further. "All my tissues, gone. They went through three boxes in a day. One student even told me he saves his snot for my class. We've got to do something about this."

We all exchange knowing looks as we chew, offering him nods and noncommittal hums of agreement. No words are needed. Our lunch break is short, and soon we'll have to disperse for duty.

I remember why I decided to eat lunch with the group today, in addition to their commiserating company. This is an intel gathering mission. Cohen and I didn't end up meeting yesterday, finding ourselves in a surprise first day of school meeting from admin. Today after school we were going to meet at our new spot, a local bookstore, to go over the murder board.

Anything I gather now can be added to our intel list, so I need something. A lead is a lead, even if I have to work with my mentee to get it. But I'm still not sure this partnership will work out.

The others are mid conversation, and I interrupt before I lose my nerve. "Speaking of food, can you believe that Mr. Anders died at a school event? Have you guys heard anything about how they're handling things?"

"Were we speaking about food?" Herald asks, glancing at the others for confirmation.

I can feel Cohen's gaze from here and don't bother checking to see what awaits me. I'm sure it's some kind of glare with annoyance thrown in. I guess I'm not as subtle as I thought?

Cohen jumps in before I can make it any worse. "Elle was probably thinking about food because her last class filmed culinary today, right?"

Crossing my fingers under the table and appreciating the fact that the culinary teacher works through lunch, I explain, "Yeah, sorry, sometimes I only think in shot lists. Downfall of being a video teacher."

I throw in what I hope is an innocent shrug for good measure.

Brittany pounces on my subject change, gesturing to the board behind her. "Speaking of the Back 2 Cool disaster, I've been getting tidbits from everyone throughout the day in between classes."

The silence envelops us as the only noise comes from the sound of wrappers and chewing.

Noticing no one is going to speak up, Brittany sighs. "I was talking to one of the English teachers who overheard one of the assistant principals with Riley the law enforcement teacher." We try to remember to include titles for the new teachers in the room until they learn all the names.

"Anyway, they said he was poisoned by something called Ethylene glycol. Or maybe it was Hemlock? Right when they said it a fight broke out and the cheering drowned it out." She looks around the room with a smile like the know-it-all student, waiting to collect her praise.

Those poisons couldn't be more different if they tried. Ethylene glycol is commonly found in antifreeze, while Hemlock would be more difficult to get ahold of and would need to be special ordered, meaning pre-meditation was at play. Only Brittany would leave me with more questions than answers.

Some shift uncomfortably, not engaging with Brittany. Though everyone's curious about what happened to Mr. Anders, she seems to forget this isn't a game and a man is dead. I'm sure some of the other teachers had his son in their classes, so no one wants to dwell on it in their free time.

Jade changes the subject. "I heard Ezra's doing his rounds the rest of this week, so be prepared for surprise observations." Everyone groans.

"Classes just started," Brittany complains.

Cohen glances around the room. "What are surprise observations?"

Brittany explains, "He'll just walk in at any time during your class and stay for about ten minutes."

Herald adds, "And he doesn't say anything, he just writes notes on his clipboard and silently judges you from afar." Brittany bumps his shoulder. "I mean, he's probably not judging us? I guess."

"He's just…" Jade starts.

"Popping in," we say in unison, mocking his tone.

"He was obsessed with us when his classroom was near us last year and was always 'popping in' to say something," I tell Cohen.

"He probably just knew he would be our AP, so he wanted to kiss up early?" Brittany says between bites.

Jade rolls her eyes. "Now he definitely doesn't kiss up to anyone. He's in AP power trip mode."

Herald sighs. "Don't worry, all APs are intense at first and chill out as they get the hang of it. Just give him a few years."

The fresh, albeit humid, mountain air whips my hair around my face in a mini tornado, causing half to stick to my lip gloss and a rogue strand to land in my eye. After that catastrophe is fixed, I have a full view of The Plot Thickens, an adorable local bookstore that continues to capture my heart. I smile to myself as I think of Cohen suggesting a coffee shop as our meeting place. Our goal is to try to not run into any students and he accidentally picked their main hangout.

Luckily for us, they don't frequent this bookstore, since it's tucked out of the way towards the back of the town square. It's a hidden gem that will give us space to work without curious eyes equipped with cell phones, speculating on why we're together outside of school.

I round the corner and my heart skips a beat as I spy the red brick storefront adorned with yellow flowers spilling out from the window box and black trim that adds just the right amount of contrast. The cheery chiming bell greets me as I step inside.

I'm early, no surprise there, so I make a beeline for my favorite section. I pass rows of colorful titles peeking out from moody green shelves that would make Joanna Gaines proud. The smell of books greets me the way no one else ever could.

When I arrive at my section I smile up at the prickly succulent that lies at the top of the shelf and the chalkboard writing that reads "Romance."

I love a good thriller, fantasy novel, or any genre really, but there is something about romance that is both comforting and exhilarating. I start to browse, on the hunt for my next read, when I feel a whoosh of air beside me. I'm expecting to find one of the usual suspects, a mom with a child strapped to her chest, or an elderly woman, but instead Cohen's chestnut hair catches the light beside me. I jump in surprise.

"Hey, you could have said something when you walked up. I was just killing time."

"Oh hey, Elle. I was just looking in my usual section," he says casually.

"Usual section? This is your usual section?" I gesture to the area of colorful spines and kissing couples dawning almost every book. Since when did he take long walks through the romance section? I mean anyone can read romance, but he doesn't seem like the target audience for these books. I would guess he'd be more interested browsing the James Patterson collection.

"Yes. Elle. Guys can read romance novels." He scoffs, grabbing a book from the shelf.

"Yeah, sorry. I didn't mean you couldn't read romance novels. I think more guys would benefit from reading them," I justify. I'm still unsure if this is one of his jokes and he's going to gotcha me any second.

He grabs a second book off the shelf in a last-minute act of determination.

"I'll be right back," he says waving his purchases in lieu of explanation.

I'm still trying to wrap my head around the fact that chill, sarcastic, and effortlessly charismatic Cohen is holding Katherine Center and Jessica Joyce novels. Regardless of what I said, I'm stunned he not only reads romance novels but has fantastic taste. Maybe there's more depth to him than I thought?

CHAPTER NINE

Cohen

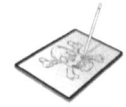

E very time. Every time I'm around Elle I somehow find a way to dig myself a little deeper. I say the wrong thing or come on too strong.

Maybe buying romance novels will be the thing that moves the needle? I trudge up to the counter, feeling her eyes on my back and I switch my weight from one foot to the other, pretending to read the back cover of my choices while I wait in line by the register.

Have I ever read a romance novel? Nope. If Elle had asked me my favorite author, would I have been able to answer? Nope. She seemed impressed when I was in that section, but I was too busy staring at her browsing that I forgot to say anything and didn't want to seem like a total idiot, so I doubled down. It was too easy to parrot the words I heard my sister drone on about at family dinner.

I ended up with two of the covers taking up permanent residence on her bookshelf. Now, I was going to read *The Bodyguard* and *You*

With a View, to be able to casually slip them into conversation with Elle.

After completing my purchase I meander around the shop until I find Elle at a table tucked into the corner of the store, a twisting ivy plant on the shelf behind her almost touching the top of her head.

She doesn't notice me approaching, engrossed in whatever research she's doing on her laptop. This seems like more of a date to me, but the set of her jaw and furious typing, tells me we aren't on the same wavelength.

All business, she looks up as I sit down, trying to tuck my knees inso they don't brush hers.

"Hey, I shared the board with you, so take a look and we'll go from there," she instructs.

Frazzled and exhausted, I try to gather the energy to focus on our task. Doing anything after school is going to take some getting used to. I grab my laptop and start to set it on the small round table, causing it to wobble.

"Elle you're going to have to move that thing over. Seriously, is that an iMac or a laptop?" I question, cursing myself for making sure we won't be in date territory today.

Elle scoffs. "It's a custom MacBook. I had to get a larger screen for better video editing."

"That's what monitors are for," I question, genuinely curious to know why she doesn't use one.

"Yeah, I know. But I have only my timeline on the monitor and use the other screen to—why am I explaining my process to you? This isn't what we came for."

She scoots it barely an inch closer to her, giving me a sliver more space. "Happy now, princess?"

"Yes, I just love balancing my laptop on the world's smallest end table," I exclaim, sarcasm dripping from my voice. I've never seen her be anything but sugary sweet to everyone else, so I can't help but feel special with the way she seems put off by me when we're not talking about school stuff.

I'm about to point out that I'm giving up my free time to help her with the case when I spy a table open up that's at least twice the size of our current predicament and pick up my laptop, rushing over to it in a mad dash to claim the better spot.

Elle hesitates, not wanting to admit defeat easily. She takes her time walking over and distributes a blue shopping bag at my feet.

"You forgot your reading material." She points out, holding up the bag I left abandoned at the foot of our old table. "Do you have the board pulled up yet?"

"Now that I can actually type without hitting the edge of the table, yes, I have the board up."

She's about to start talking, but I can't help myself as I interrupt her.

"Oh, and you don't have to call me a princess to tell me I'm pretty." I smirk.

Caught off guard, I can tell she's trying not to smile but fails miserably.

Giving into her laugh, she quips, "Whatever. I'm pretty sure if it takes you that long to think of a comeback then it doesn't count."

She clears her throat to wipe away any trace of humor in her voice. "I've been thinking about it all day and I can't figure out who would want to target Mr. Anders. If you look in the middle of the page, you can see I have a sticky note of what we know, so as we learn things, we can make notes."

Trying to switch into business mode with the same efficiency, I question, "So you're sure he was the target because the PTA moms always make him a special dish? Out of the hundreds of parents, you're sure he is the only one who eats it?"

"Yes, I'm positive. The vegan gluten free mac and cheese only has the same three spoonful's gone each time, and it's made with white cheese sauce, so I know his plate is the only one I ever see it on. And the moms' brag about catering to all food allergies/preferences and use him as an example at all the event prep meetings." She clears her throat. "Sorry, used him as an example."

My chest tightens at the sound of pain coating her words. "Tell me more about how you knew him."

She looks down at her lap, fidgeting with her hands. "Even though I didn't have his son, he was a friend of one of my students and Mr. Anders was at every event I worked for duty." She smiles to herself and slowly looks up to meet my eyes. "He would always chat with us and take our photos for the school website and general PTA stuff. You know how everyone always wants you to say cheese?"

"Sure," I agree.

She huffs a laugh. "Well, he would tell us to say please." Her lips curl in a sad smile taking a deep breath before continuing. "When I asked him about it, he said it's something his son said when he was little and it just stuck." She wipes at an errant tear that escapes down her cheek, clearing her throat. "I just don't get it."

A fresh wave of resolve hums through my bones. "That's why we're going to solve this."

"We're gonna try," she counters.

"Nope, I have a good feeling about this," I declare. I want to reach for her hand, but I don't want to freak her out, so I change the subject instead.

"So, um. Do we have to go to all the prep meetings?" I groan inwardly. Why was that the first thing that came to mind? I could've transitioned our conversation in a million directions and I defaulted back to school.

"No, remember when I told you I was on fifty committees? The PTA event planning was one of them. This is why you shouldn't sign up for too much this year."

"Why are you so sure he was poisoned? What if he had a heart attack or there's a different cause of death?" I wonder aloud. Maybe we're looking at this from the wrong angle.

"He made these choking sounds, a few minutes after I watched him eat a few bites of mac and cheese."

Playing devil's advocate, I chime in, "But was that the only thing on his plate? It could have been another dish that did him in if he was poisoned."

"It was the only thing on his plate, because it's the only thing he can eat with his allergy. And I just know it was poisoned. I feel it in my gut." Grimacing, she adds somberly, "No pun intended."

"Ok, we'll go with your theory until we have an official cause after the autopsy. How are we gonna get that information anyway?" I sigh. "I doubt Riley will just offer it up."

"You're right. I guess we'll just have to find a way." She shrugs, focusing back on her laptop." Anyway, I've started digging into Mr. Anders' Facebook, but I need you to comb through the PTA Facebook page. We're looking for anything, no matter how small. Did he head up a specific event? Is there a snarky parent comment? Literally anything."

"Ok, what was his role?" I wonder.

"Historian. He is —was a professional photographer, so he always took photos of all the events." She swallows hard, shaking her head in an effort to physically make herself stop the thoughts I can practically see starting to make their way to the front of her mind.

I start on my task but decide to try to take her mind off the guilt that washes over her face. Obviously, I know that even though I made Elle abandon her post at the Back 2 Cool event, it's not our fault Mr. Anders is dead. It's the person who poisoned him. If helping her with this case will ease her burden and give her closure, that's good enough for me.

"Why is everyone wearing that?" I ask as I rotate my laptop so she can see the picture in question.

This seems to draw Elle out of her head a bit as she laughs. "That's dress like a student day. Where the parents and teachers dressed like students. It was a fundraiser to raise money for the Scholars of Tomorrow fund."

"Scholars of Tomorrow?"

"Yeah, the PTA president, Pat McPatterson, started this fund that gets pooled together at the end of each year to award one student a full-ride scholarship. Last year was the first full year, and the student is at NYU for free," Elle explains.

"Pat McPatterson. Did his parents have a vendetta against him or something?"

"That's what you got from all that? No, Pat was his mother's maiden name, and McPatterson just happened to be his dad's last name. He's so used to explaining, he tells everyone up front now to save time."

"Do you have a story behind your name?" I ask Elle.

She glances up at me, the first time she's met my eyes since we moved tables. "Nope, my parents just liked the name. What about you?"

"I have three siblings, and because my parents couldn't agree on a name, my dad picked the first one, my mom the second, and so on. By the time they got to me, my mom saw Cohen and went with it. It just so happens to be the same name as my dad's college roommate/arch nemesis, so you could say it has served me well since day one." I look back at my computer, trying to brush it off. "Don't get me wrong, my dad's great, but he still winces sometimes when he says my name."

"So is there a no-take backs policy? When your mom found that out, didn't she want to pick something else?"

"It was on the birth certificate already and no one wanted to put in the extra work to get it fixed. By the time they got around to it, I would have been able to spell my name already. That's just what happens when you have multiple siblings. Some stuff just falls through the cracks." I use more force than necessary to punch the right click button on my trackpad.

She starts to close the screen of my laptop, forcing me to look up.

"Cohen, I'm sorry. It's not too late to change your name now. You don't have to live with it forever." She sucks in a breath ready to continue, but I cut her off.

"Really, it's fine. Do you pull this guidance counselor routine on your students?" I question, hoping to change the subject.

Realizing I'm done with this line of questioning, she gives me a halfhearted grin. "Of course, how else am I going to get to the bottom of the case of the missing SD cards?

But you'll find out, counselor is practically in our job description. Most students don't have anyone to talk to, so if you take a minute to get to know them, sometimes they'll tell you more than you bargained for."

"Like what?"

"Their favorite chip flavor, what their siblings did to piss them off that morning, and sometimes, their plans for the future, or the dream major they would pick if they didn't feel like their parents would judge them for it, you never know."

At that, we continue to work in companionable silence, to the ambient sounds of flipping book pages, and light conversation between customers acting as our soundtrack.

Until I take a deep inhale as I bump up an image from the Back 2 Cool event. "Hey, I think I might have something."

Quicker than I can turn my monitor her way, she's up out of her seat, and I can feel Elle's hand tentatively cover my shoulder blade as she leans in to see my screen. I fight to keep my shoulders even, as I don't want to spook her with too much movement and remind her where her hand is currently resting, even though it feels as if it's burning a hole in the sleeve of my button down.

"It's a photo of the PTA moms." Elle huffs, disappointment thickly clouding her voice.

Speaking softer, not having to strain to be heard over the shop noise, I point out.

"Yeah, but look at the photographer. You can see the mop and bucket next to the table, and his green uniform is reflected in the punch bowl."

"Woah, you're right. It's the janitor, Mr. Joseph. We may actually have our first real lead," she says with a smile spreading on her face.

"You're more observant than I gave you credit for," she compliments, clearly impressed.

"During library time I always went right for the *Where's Waldo* books, so I guess you could say I have an eye for detail. I knew those skills were transferrable," I say with an underhanded fist pump.

She laughs in spite of herself. "Well, now we're getting somewhere. Our next step is to question Mr. Josephs and see if he witnessed anything at the food table."

"Jinkee's, I think we found a clue," I manage.

"Velma, I really hope you won't say that every time we get a new lead," she chides, smile still intact.

"We need to come up with our own catchphrase then," I suggest.

"That can be your domain, Cohen."

And to think she was about to kick me out of the duo, and now I'm in charge. Of a catchphrase, but still, that's progress. I got her to laugh, found a lead, and got a task. Does that mean I'm winning her over?

CHAPTER TEN

Elle

"Ok, who wants to go first?" I say with mock enthusiasm, hoping that one brave soul will volunteer. Ezra the new AP just did one of his pops-ins and is standing in the back of the room with his trademark clipboard in hand.

At first, my request is met with silence as I stare at the other faces in the circle, willing someone to go first. I don't need my first observation with Ezra to fail epically. It's our first pitch meeting in Video 1, with the sophomores, and I'm praying someone will put me out of my misery.

We all sit in a semicircle, true newsroom style, as we drum up ideas for their first videos that will help round out the student news program produced by the seniors. I'm about to start calling on students, when one hand shoots up. It's Mia, a student I had in my intro class last year.

"I'll go. So, I heard the health classes aren't doing the baby project this year, and I want to know why? They've been doing that project since my sister was a freshman, and she graduated a few years ago."

"I like it, what kind of b-roll will you film?"

Mia taps her foot, lost in thought. "I could get footage of the plastic babies in the storage closet, and a shot of students holding the baby, for when I talk about the use of them in the past."

"That sounds great, and to get more coverage, you can get some shots of the teacher teaching and students learning that can play when you talk about the project that takes its place," I suggest.

"Oh, good idea. Thanks Ms. Dannon."

"Of course!" I jot the idea down on my sheet.

"Anyone else?" I'm met with silence until I clarify.

"Remember, you won't receive a pitch grade if you don't pitch an idea."

Seven hands magically catapult at the mention of grades. This is what I like about the sophomores. They still care about their grades. This trick wouldn't work on most seniors.

Teddy starts excitedly when I nod at him to present. "So I want to do a piece on how Lebron James has influenced basketball."

"The basketball team here, or in general?" I question.

"In general. The entire game of basketball," Teddy replies confidently. Before other students can object to his statement, I cut in. "Do you know Lebron?"

The students laugh. Teddy frowns. "No."

"Then how are you going to get an interview with him? And film b-roll of him playing basketball?"

Teddy takes a moment to contemplate how to make this happen as I go into my explanation.

"Also, remember we want it to be newsworthy. So why now? For example, if the basketball team here decided to implement some techniques from Lebron that put them on a winning streak this season, then you have a story. And an excuse to talk about Lebron."

"Oooh, that makes sense. Ok, my backup idea is debate team."

"What about debate team?" I prompt.

"They have a district meet against their biggest rival coming up. I could get a few wide, medium, and tight shots of them practicing. My friend says it gets pretty intense, and I can interview the debate coach and a member."

"That sounds like a great idea! As long as you don't interview your friend."

He looks up affronted. "Why not?"

"Because you need practice interviewing people you don't know."

He gives me a sly smile. "But what if I did it anyway. How would you know I interviewed my friend?"

I'm about to respond as one of my seniors comes in to grab a camera. "Oh, she'll know. Trust me from experience, you don't want to have to go and refilm that interview."

I'll just chalk it up to what the students call my teacher magic. I won't tell them that I wiped all the SD cards, and heard them joking around with their friends off camera.

Teddy shakes his head in agreement, seemingly placated by the response.

What can I say? Seniors give the best advice. The rest of the meeting continues, making it glaringly obvious who came in with ideas, and who has to pick from my list of options. I think my backup list for those who run out of ideas is inspired, but they've often said they're boring.

Which actually makes it a stronger classroom management tool to come to class prepared. A win's a win. The bell rings, and I sigh in relief, knowing we only have a few more to get to tomorrow. It's exhausting until they get the hang of it.

Ezra stops by to chat and ask about some students we had in common last year. Hopefully small talk with him will earn me a good spot in his book. I'm almost home free until he asks, "So, how's it going with Cohen as your mentee? Is he adjusting to teaching ok?"

Well, I'm obviously not going to complain that they could've put me with someone less distracting, but I can't admit to that. Every time I interact with Cohen, I feel like something dumb comes out of my mouth before I can take it back. But by the lack of flirty and or cheesy things he says to me, I can't help thinking it may be mutual.

I settle on; "Great, his industry experience makes him a hit with the kids already." Hopefully he won't notice my voice has raised an octave.

"Oh good! I'm observing him next period. I can't wait to see him in action." The man throws up finger guns and walks out of the room.

Letting the fake smile plastered on my face drop, I gather my papers, plop them on my desk, walking out into the hallway to find a certain teacher already waiting for me.

To anyone else, Cohen would look like the picture of calm and collected. He is leaning against the wall, one shoe touching the wall, arms crossed. Maybe I've gone full detective already, but I notice the way a few strands of hair stick up as if he's been running his fingers through them in frustration, and he's tapping his thumb against his forearm in a steady rhythm.

"What's up?" I try to sound casual, but probably fail.

"We're really doing this," he whispers.

"What?"

"Questioning Mr. Joseph. Today. After school."

"Yep, that's kind of how sleuthing works. Now drop it before Riley hears you." I glance back at the door.

"Paranoid much?"

"Seriously, his room is right there." I nod behind me.

"By the way, Ezra is going to do a pop-in observation in your class after lunch."

"Really? The class after lunch. Is he hazing me or something?" Cohen asks, already exasperated.

I hold my hands up in defense. "Hey, you've been warned."

I start making my way towards our lunch spot and he follows.

I start walking quickly but force myself to slow when I spot the mop bucket outside my room. I try to get my eye twitch under control as I spot Mr. Joseph spraying industrial cleaner and cloth directly onto the iMac screen as he wipes them down and prepares myself to focus on the task at hand. Cohen slowly walks in behind me.

"Hey, Mr. Josephs, how's your school year been?"

He barely glances my way as he continues down the row of computers.

"Fine, we've only had three puking incidents, and a collage project." He shutters at the thought. As if the paper scraps from a collage are infinitely worse than the puke.

"But it's only the first week of school," Cohen says incredulously.

"Yeah, and that's good for us," he clarifies.

Is it the computer screen glow, or does he look extra pale? Plus, he's normally not the most social, but he won't meet our eyes.

Trying to ease into the conversation, I start, "Sorry, I forgot to introduce you. Mr. Joseph, this is Cohen."

"We've already met," Cohen explains.

"Yep, someone was trying to change the ink in the copy room and somehow got ink everywhere." He shakes his head slowly in disbelief.

I jump in. "Well, we're lucky we have someone like you to help us out. This school wouldn't run without you to fix things. And we appreciate all the long hours you put in."

He nods in appreciation, clearing his throat.

"In fact, you even took pictures of the PTA moms for the Back 2 Cool event, right?"

"Yep," he says quietly, intently focusing on scrubbing a spot from the computer screen.

Cohen speaks up, "Did you happen to see anyone else around the food table around that time?"

"There was someone there. I was trying to get a punch stain from the floor over by the table."

Cohen treads slowly. "Did you see them or hear their voice?"

"I had my headphones in and I didn't look at them. No reason to," he says quickly.

Mr. Joseph jumps to a computer out of order, so he can put his back to us. Taking the hint, I grab my teacher bag and gather up my cups.

"Thanks for your help, Mr. Joseph," I sing-song and nod to Cohen to follow me out.

We stop at his room to grab his stuff.

As he's shutting and locking his own door, he hisses, "Why did you stop our progress? We were finally getting somewhere."

"He was shutting down and wasn't going to give us anything else. I think he's hiding something," I reason.

"Was it the way he wouldn't look at us the entire time, or the short answers that clued you in?" Cohen grabs his bag with too much force, and beelines for his door.

I stay by his desk and talk at his back. "Hey, don't gripe with me. We're still figuring out this detective thing. Suspects aren't just going to pour their hearts out to us because we ask."

His pinched expression softens a bit. "Sorry, I was taking out my frustration on you and that's not fair. You're right, this was the first of what I'm sure will be many interrogations."

"I think this qualifies as a fact-finding mission, not full-on interrogation. I didn't even use my teacher look or voice, so I think he got off easy," I speculate.

Cohen laughs with me. "True, power like that is a gift and a cur—"

"You've branched out to Monk now?"

"Oh yeah, I had to broaden my research. Who knew that show was so addicting?" he exclaims.

"Literally everyone. That's why it won like four Emmy's and a Golden Globe." I smile in spite of myself. We walk through the hallway,

Changing the subject, I ask, "So how'd the observation go?"

Cohen grimaces. "It was fine, I guess. I had to tell like three students to put their phones away."

"Did they?"

"Yeah, instantly. But they had them out." He rubs his neck in embarrassment, not meeting my eyes.

I nudge him with my shoulder in solidarity. "Sure, but the fact that they put them away quickly with one warning shows good classroom management. Things will always go wrong, but they're looking at how you handle them and how your students respond to you."

He softens, "I haven't thought about it that way. Thanks."

I nod and we start the trek to the teacher parking lot. It feels like a step forward on the mentoring front, but it's too early to tell.

I'm just minding my own business, sauteing the veggies for our dinner, when Jade bursts into the room blowing on her freshly painted mint green nails.

"So Nancy Drew, what'd you and the Hardy Boy do today?" Jade challenges, quirking her brow, flashing a grin my way.

Does everyone in my life consume the same revolving hamster wheel of crime media?

"I get enough detective references from Cohen, so if you start too, I'll spontaneously combust," I lament, dramatically waving the spatula around, probably sprinkling vegetable bits all over our kitchen floor.

"Hmmm, it sounds like you two are getting close. I heard a few of my kids talking about you two the other day." She casually throws in while inspecting her nails.

"Woah, what now?" I'm trying not to let my blood pressure rise, but this doesn't seem like it will be about how awesome our classes are.

"Yep, they were talking about how you two always flirt with each other in the hallway." She glances my way, knowing that I'm crawling out of my skin in embarrassment.

I look at her affronted, spatula resting on my clavicle, until I come to and realize how gross that is and chuck it in the sink with a huff.

"How are you so calm about this?" I ask.

"Hey, I'm not the one flirting in the hallway." She puts her hands up in defense. Ugh, was I actually flirting in the hallway?

At my bug eyes, she continues, "Elle relax. I'm messing with you. So what if you are talking to a colleague in a manner that some would consider flirtatious? Can I make the point again that there is literally nothing stopping you from dating another teacher. So why aren't you?"

"And why am I explaining this to you for the millionth time, Jade. I can't date Cohen, for so many reasons."

"Which are?" She patiently waits for me to explain.

"If we tried it and it didn't work, I would have to walk by his classroom every day," I reason.

"I could convince AP Ezra to let me switch back to my old room next to you at semester. Next."

Jade looks at me with a bored expression, and motions for me to continue.

"Fine, it would look unprofessional and after ground zero our first year, I can't afford to take another hit."

"You're worried about your reputation at a school where Herald shows movies to literally every class, five first years quit yesterday, and that student flushed Cheetos down the toilet, backing up the entire third floor's plumbing and it's only the first week of school? Admin has enough to worry about and they aren't sitting around contemplating your job performance. You're gonna have to do better than that. Next."

Saving the grand finale for last, I hit Jade with: "Ok, what about the fact that Cohen is so confusing. One day, he is seemingly flirting with me, but how many other teachers does he charm? I mean, I've seen the way the other first years look at him. He must have women giving him their phone numbers left and right. What if it's all a joke to him?"

Jade chimes in, exasperation lacing her words, "It's not. And I'm sure he's helping the other teachers solve a case and hanging on to their every word. Oh wait. That's just you."

I huff and retort, "You don't know how he acts around other women."

Her eyes widen. "Do you?"

I shuffle my feet, not meeting her eyes. "No."

She looks at me with a smile. "Maybe you shouldn't make judgements about him until you give him a chance. I don't see what one date could hurt. It's not as if I'm asking you to marry him. Plus, you could use a little excitement in your life. Maybe he's the person to get you out of your comfort zone."

I'm speechless and in true Jade fashion, she takes this time to gloat in my face as only a true friend can. She makes it sound so easy. Like we can just walk away after one date. Like it won't make things complicated.

"You're not allowed to make excuses around me, Elle. My reasoning was so sound, you can admit I won and you need to give him a chance. To celebrate my victory, I get first dibs and will be eating a majority of the water chestnuts, and the sugar snap peas." Jade shimmies her way over to the pan. I groan in frustration, because she knows that the water chestnuts and sugar snap peas are my favorite. I try to get in between her and the pan, but she hip checks me out of the way and collects her prize. *Well played, Jade.*

Chapter Eleven

Cohen

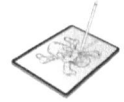

"M ister?" Landon, a student with a pension for questions, asks in the middle of class.

"It's Mr. Sinclair, but yes, Landon?" I sigh. Is it that difficult to remember my name?

"Where's Maximus?" he asks with genuine concern. Was he sniffing one of my dry erase markers again? I thought I locked those in my desk.

"Huh?" I ask, caught off guard.

Several students try to muffle their laughter, sputtering loudly.

Addison, throws me a bone. "Ya know? Because you look like Flynn Rider?"

"From Tangled?" I clarify.

The class nods empathically.

"Has no one told you that before?" they ask in disbelief.

I have a flashback to my brothers putting me in a headlock while screaming, "Rider, where's Rapenzel," in my ear.

"Nope, never," I deadpan.

Another student tilts their head in concentration. "I don't know, I'm getting Sebastin Stan?"

They continue with their conversation as if I'm not standing here. "The First Avenger?"

"Definitely," the other confirms.

My gaze travels around the room, stopping on a student with Captain America stickers all over his laptop. He nods in approval.

"Orrrrr, Roddy from Flushed Away?"

The class erupts in laughter, one student falling out of her seat.

A teacher walks by, slowing down as she reaches the windows of my room, giving passersby a full view of my class, an eyebrow raised in judgement.

Great, I'm sure the whole hallway can hear us.

Having humored them long enough, I decide it's time to get class back on track and pick up where I left off.

At lunch, Elle and Jade stop in their tracks, but I don't notice, too preoccupied staring at myself in my phone camera. I look side to side, trying to see the resemblance.

Jade walks over to one side and lightly places her hand on my arm. "What did they say?"

Elle moves to the other side, placing her hand on the other arm. Ignoring the way my stomach flips as she squeezes in solidarity, I respond, "How'd you know?"

Elle laughs. "They do this to all guy teachers."

Jade nods. "They love comparing you to characters that they'll use to roast you with for the rest of the year. Who'd you get?"

I mumble, "Flynn Rider."

Elle breaks into uncontrollable laughter, and Jade's cackle threatens to blow my ear drums.

Jade manages to say through weezes, "You're good," reaching into her pocket and handing Elle a crumpled wad of cash.

"Wait, you bet on this?" I ask, astonished. What else have they bet on?

Jade's laughter finally peeters out. She replies hoarsely, "Yeah, I had money on Roddy from Flushed Away, but your girl had Flynn Rider."

I can feel the flush creeping up my neck at Jade's "my girl" comment. I should be so lucky.

"At least you don't have to worry about a Halloween costume," Elle chimes in, oblivious to my reaction.

I snap out of it, "Absolutely not."

Jade chides, "Oh come on. Just think about it." The girls share a smile, which makes me wonder if they've talked about me outside of school.

Later that night I'm failing to focus on the task at hand and it's taking me twice as long. I had falsely assumed as a teacher I wouldn't be the one with homework, but as I pick at my food while working on the laptop at the dining table, I realize how very wrong I was. The glowing screen is feeling more like a digital set of handcuffs as I near the end of my nightly tasks. I have been grading student essays on the history of font types and am finally finishing up some sleuthing work for Elle.

As she put it, we needed to make some progress and fill out the murder board. While we know someone poisoned Mr. Anders food, we haven't added any additional suspects. Was our investigation stalemating before we even got it off the ground?

Ren brings me out of my thoughts with a jolt. "Earth to Cohen, you've got to put that computer away. You're stressing me out."

I sigh and shut the laptop, thankful for an excuse to take a break.

"You're right. I just can't get everything done during the day."

He looks at me over his glasses. "You need better time management."

I laugh bitterly, silently cussing him out in my head. "It's hard to have better time management when you have a room full of fourteen-year-olds, just waiting for a chance to stab the keyboards with their pencils, swap all the mice until they find the 'perfect' one, and stick gum under the tables. Which I still haven't seen them actually do it, they're gum ninjas. But I have the evidence to prove it," I finish my side tangent with a sigh.

"Point taken. I don't know how you do it." He shakes his head in horror.

"Neither do I," I lament.

With that, Ren puts his dish in the sink and leaves me to flounder with my thoughts. Done for the night, I put up my own plate and meander to the couch. The Bodyguard is staring me down from the coffee table where I threw it down after our trip to the bookstore. I grab it, open the first page, and settle in.

CHAPTER TWELVE

Cohen

I step over the threshold into Elle's classroom to the sound of laughter. In our meeting at the beginning of school, much to Jade and I's protests, Elle thought it would be a great idea to swap classes for a day and teach a lesson to each other's students, so that's what we're trying today. As I walk further into the room, the students come into full view. They're all watching her with rapt attention as Elle has both her thumbs and pointer fingers out, creating a makeshift, pantomime camera. "Pan left," she yells, and everyone, including her, tilt their hips slowly to the left, dragging their imaginary cameras with them. "Dolly in," she exclaims, as they all take a few steps forward, keeping their cameras as steady as possible.

Noticing my presence, she looks over and steps to the side. "Hey, they're ready for you."

"What's this?" I ask, nodding towards her hands.

"Oh, this is the camera movement version of Simon Says. We're still getting the hang of the vocab, and what it actually means when filming," she states brightly.

"Ms. Dannon? My camera's getting heavy," a student says, pretending to hold a heavy object.

"Mine too!" another student objects.

Elle snaps to attention, "Right, cameras down everyone."

A collective sigh of relief fills the room as the class puts down their imaginary cameras.

"Remember, be good for Mr. Sinclair, and if you're not..."

A student finishes, "We'll be on SD card wiping duty," scrunching up their nose, shuttering a little.

Elle nods, content with their answer, and makes her way to my classroom.

The reality of my situation, in charge of a class I know nothing about with a group of students I don't know is slowly hitting me as they wait for me to start.

After a second of indecision, I snap into action, wordlessly pulling up a PowerPoint on the screen.

"Today, we'll be going over the principles of design. They influence every design you'll create and give you a rulebook to start with. Eventually it will all become second nature."

I point at the screen. "What do you think about this poster? What elements look good? Think color, font, layout, etc."

A hand shoots in the air and silent relief floods my brain. This is a group of sophomores, who are normally quicker to answer than freshmen. I nod at them to speak.

"So, once we get done with the PowerPoint what game are we playing?" they ask exasperated.

"Game?" I ask. Is this a trick question?

Another student pips up without raising their hand.

"Yeah, when we finish the lesson, Ms. Dannon has a game or activity ready for us to practice."

The others all nod in agreement. A game? Since when was a prerequisite for lesson planning a game? Hoping they'll magically forget about this if I keep talking, I just turn back to the board.

"Ok, let's get to it then. The first rule of design is..." and I continued with my speech/lesson. Overall, it went pretty well. The students paid attention for the most part and answered all my questions. We even got into a mini discussion after one very divisive example that had the class split 50/50 on whether it qualified as good design.

The bell was ringing before I knew it and as Elle glides back into her room, she stops to ask a student. "Are you designing your own short film posters from now on?" The girl responds with a shrug.

"It was fine. I learned what good design looks like, but we never got to put it into practice. Don't hold your breath. See you tomorrow, Ms. Dannon." She smiles at Elle walking past her on her way out the door.

Elle had to give me a pep talk and we ended up eating lunch together in her room, because I was too distraught to face the lunch crew. As if that weren't embarrassing enough; the next day, Brad, who always has a guaranteed scowl on his face says, "Can that teacher come back to our class again?"

"Why, what'd you do?" I question, trying to figure out what hypnotic spell Elle casts over the teens while simultaneously choosing to remain unoffended by the comment.

Jules, another student pipes up, "We went over some tips for cell phone videography."

Brad finished, "And then we had a scavenger hunt in the hallway. And I won."

Jules glares his way. "Our TEAM won."

Their bickering is interrupted by a few students giggling into their phones. I cut in, "Have we learned nothing? Phones away or you take them to the office," I reprimand, using my best stern teacher voice. The cell phone thing was already getting old for how early in the year it was.

With the rumble of a teen symphony of sighs and eye rolls, they reluctantly put them away, to stare back at me, arms crossed. Determined to get us back on track, I start on our lesson today, forgetting to ask them what they were all looking at on their phones. Probably just another viral something or another.

Before I know it, my butt is squeezed back in a student desk with the other teachers at lunch. I stare down at my PB&J, magically wishing it into something better. No luck. I need to be more like Ren and prep my meals. Maybe one day my roommate's tendencies will rub off on me.

I'm so caught up in my thoughts, I almost don't notice the way the other teachers in the room are staring Elle and I down. It feels like they know something we don't, and by that gossipy teacher Brittany's sinister smile, I wonder if we're somehow the topic of her latest findings.

Elle breaks the silence. "Ok, what is it? Why are you looking at us like that?"

She motions between us as if we're one unit.

Jade waltzes in, always the last one to join the group. "Elle, on a scale from one to ten, how much are you freaking out right now?"

Exasperated and about to lose it, she practically screeches, "What should I be freaking out about?" Based on the shock on the other teachers' faces, it looks like we're the only ones not in on the joke.

Wordlessly, Jade unlocks her phone and hands it to Elle. I lean over in my seat and tap her shoulder, so I can see too. A squeak of shock escapes from Elle as we look at an Instagram account with the handle @TeamDannonSinclair. There are only three photos so far, but Elle clicks on the first photo to view the caption.

I snort and recite a couple of the captions to the group, accompanying the stalker like photos of us talking in the hallway: "We see you, hashtag Dannon Sinclair. And we ship it, winking emoji."

Herald looks up from his lunch. "What's a ship?"

Brittany lets out a light laugh as she explains, "Ship is short for relationship. When there are two people you think should be together, you ship them and hope they get the message." She aims a pointed glance our way.

Herald shakes his head. "I stopped trying to keep up with the jargon years ago. It'll change before I can remember it."

Jade nods. "To be fair, Herald, if you ever used any of those terms, the kids would call you cringe anyway."

He groans. "I'm not even going to ask what cringe means."

Brittany chimes in, "That's why it can be fun to use it when they least expect it. They might be rolling their eyes, but at least they're listening."

A chorus of synchronized mumbles fill the room.

I continue to the next one, showcasing a photo, where we're caught mid-laugh standing next to Riley. "Who needs fiction when we have hashtag Team Dannon Sinclair in real life, heart emoji, book emoji."

Face drained of all color, Elle shoves the phone in my hand, stuffs the contents of her lunch back in her lunchbox, smooshing her PB&J,

otherwise known as the official sandwich of broke, tired teachers everywhere, and makes a beeline out of the room without a word.

Trying not to take it personally that she's upset about being shipped with me, I pack up my sad excuse of a lunch and head out too. "See you guys tomorrow," I mumble, trying to brush off the awkwardness.

As I shut the door, I catch Brittany's comment, "Seems like the rumors might not be false after all," with a tinny laugh.

Even though I'm walking away, I can hear Jade telling her off at the other end of the hall. I smile to myself, thankful for another person on Elle's side.

Her door is open, so I tentatively step inside, announcing myself, so she isn't freaked out.

"Hey, it's me." I shut the door behind me so ears of the teenage variety won't catch our conversation.

She just groans, her head down on her desk, hair splayed over her folded arms, covering her face.

I try to lighten the mood, even though my pride has taken more than a few hits over the course of the day.

"Is being 'shipped' with me really that bad? I can be a great fake boyfriend, I promise." I hold up the scout's honor sign in vain, since Elle still has her head down and doesn't even notice.

She slowly pulls her head up in slow motion, eyes watery. "No, Cohen. I didn't mean—I wasn't thinking—that wasn't my intention," she finishes.

A beat passes before she continues. "Having something out like that is going to ruin the credibility I've spent years building. What if admin, or the school board, or parents see that? I work so hard to give the kids a meaningful learning experience, but they're all going to remember me as that video teacher who dated her mentee."

Feeling like the biggest, self-centered jerk in the world, I counter, "Or they could remember you as the teacher who solved a murder between classes. That's Jessica Fletcher level stuff."

She huffs out a real laugh for the first time all afternoon. "She was a criminology professor, so she had a more flexible schedule to interrogate suspects, but yeah I guess you're right."

As more color settles into her features she asks, "In all your research, have you listened to any podcasts?"

Feeling like I'm failing a pop quiz, I truthfully answer, "No, but I seriously doubt there's anything I could get from those that I can't get from Mrs. Fletcher."

She laughs without reservation this time, slowly returning to her normal demeanor."Well, if you change your mind, you have to try Serial. Sarah Koenig is my spirit animal and an actual journalist who solves things with evidence and facts."

As if an actual light bulb materializes and illuminates her features, Elle clearly gets an idea.

"What is it, E?" I ask, impatient to know what she came up with.

Her eyebrows scrunch together as she tries to ignore the use of the nickname and vocalizes her train of thought. "When Sarah hits a wall, she looks back at her files and does some investigating."

"Ok," I answer, still not connecting the dots.

"Meaning we need to call an emergency meeting at the bookstore today and figure out where our investigation should go next. Are you free?"

I was not free. I was supposed to be helping my brother wallpaper his bedroom. But there's no way I was telling Elle that.

"Sure, same spot?" I agree without hesitation.

"Of course, maybe you'll be tempted to add another book to your collection." She smiles innocently.

She is never going to let me live that down.

"It's a date, E," I say and walk out of the room before she can refute my answer. Quickly sending a text to my brother letting him know I had an emergency school related meeting that I have to attend. I mean, Elle and I might talk about school while we're there, so that counts as a meeting right?

CHAPTER THIRTEEN

Elle

S itting almost shoulder to shoulder with a certain graphic design teacher has me thinking about the last time we were sitting at The Plot Thickens fighting over table space. This time, we agree to work on my computer and look on together. As I pull up the murder board on my color-coded Google drive, I decide to make conversation. Starting with the thing I'm best at talking about. Books.

"What part are you at?" I question.

"Of what?" Cohen asks.

"Your book. Which one did you start first?" I wonder, still half expecting him to confess he was bluffing the whole time and returned them the next day or something.

"Oh, I started The Bodyguard. I got to the part where she's getting that Ms. Congeniality style makeover to go undercover."

My face must give me away, because he smirks. I squeak out, "I love that part," as the Murder Board loads on the screen.

Realization slaps me in the face. "Woah, wait a minute. You've seen Ms. Congeniality?" I ask incredulously.

Smiling, he confesses, "Isn't that what sisters are for?" I laugh and he continues.

"She was a remote hog, and I never stood a chance. I've also seen Legally Blonde more times than I can count. But I don't want to talk about it." He concedes, brushing me off.

"I definitely want to talk about it." I counter.

His smile grows wider. "Wait, did you think I wasn't going to read it? They're on my bookshelf with the other books."

"Well, now I want to know what's on your bookshelf," I retort.

"You're welcome anytime," he tells me with a smile.

I roll my eyes at his insinuation. "Ugh, I didn't mean like that. You should just take a picture of it or something."

"Nope, it's just one of those things you have to see in person," he says, not letting this go.

"Whatever, let's get back to the board." I nod towards the screen. "What we're actually supposed to be accomplishing?"

"E, you know we can have a conversation that doesn't accomplish anything," he says innocently. He knows exactly what he's doing.

"Yeah, I know. But every time we do that you throw me off," I say, caught off guard.

Once I realize I basically just admitted something, defeat or admiration, I can't tell which; I don't want to look him in the eye. Deciding to rip off the band aid and get it over with, I glance up at him. He's looking at me with the most genuine smile I've ever seen on his face. It's not his usual smirk.

Crap. Even I have to admit, it's a really good smile. Objectively speaking of course. In an unfortunate turn of events, I smile back before I can tamp down my jaw muscles.

We won't get anything done if I don't get us back on track. We're co-workers. He's my mentee.

Letting my smile melt off my face like a fade to black transition, I turn away from Cohen and tapping my screen, I say, "Ok, so we ruled out Mr. Joseph." I add a gold star next to his name and photo on the murder board.

"This means we've ruled him out," I reason.

Cohen shifts his body away from me to crane his neck to the side to glance my way.

"A gold star. Really?"

"Yes. If we don't give ourselves a gold star every now and then, who will?" I shrug, continuing, "It's like, gold star, you're not a murder. Yay you!"

"Yay you? The bar is really low these days." He snickers, but shifts back to his previous position by my side, seemingly agreeing with my methods.

"I'm sure that's exactly what Riley does on his murder board too. In fact, the police station probably rivals kindergarten teachers in gold star stock." He bumps my shoulder lightly with his.

"Oh, shut up. Did you have any luck finding any other suspects?"

He sighs. "Nope, I keep coming up empty. You?"

I share his forlorn expression. "No, but Sarah Koenig gave me an idea. She once went into this old basement and spent hours looking through files when she couldn't find anything online. I think we need to look at documents of the autopsy variety."

"Great idea, we can confirm the type of poison which could have a connection to the killer. But if we submit a Freedom of Information Act request for that legally, Riley will know we're snooping, since we have to sign our name at the bottom."

I look at him, trying to gauge the level he's willing to sneak around. "Orrrr... We could take a peek without his knowledge."

His nose scrunches and his eyebrows pinch as he utters, "Who are you, E? That sounds like something I'd suggest, and you'd fight me on."

I shift in my squeaky seat, causing a few patrons to look in our direction. "I know, but we're at a stalemate and I don't have any other ideas on how to get us out of it. We just need a reason to be in the office in his classroom, and then I can get into his file cabinet."

"A, you probably need a key for that cabinet, and B, why don't you just have the kids film a video about his class and 'supervise.'"

Woah, that's genius. I brighten at his suggestion. "Ok, that's actually pretty smart. And our file cabinet keys are universal, so mine will open it," I say.

"I'm not going to ask how you know that," he states.

"Yeah, we don't talk about the detention incident anymore," I reply solemnly.

"Noted. So... you're only looking for the autopsy report?" he questions.

"That and I want to see if I can snap a copy of the witness list. Mr. Joseph mentioned someone else was there." I tap my fingers on the table, lost in thought.

"And we're gonna use process of elimination and talk to all the witnesses?" Cohen guesses.

"Exactly! You know, it would be the perfect time to use our catch phrase, what was it again?" I question with a knowing smile.

Cohen levels me a glare, clearly not amused. "Genius takes time, I'm not quite there yet." *He's taking this really seriously.* I can't wait to see what he comes up with.

I'm in my natural state, aka, teacher mode as I run off a mental check-list with the students before we walk over to film the Riley video. It turns out finding a student to use the idea for a video was surprisingly easy as the well of ideas are already starting to run dry. We're in that awkward period. The newness of the start of the year has worn off, but activities and sports haven't really gotten underway with anything newsworthy yet.

"Camera body?" I call.

"Check." Carter answers.

"Lenses?"

"Check," Anaia responds.

"Mics?"

The zipper makes a loud sound as the silence is broken and shuffling ensues.

"Check," Carter sighs.

"And tripod?"

Anaia holds it up in lieu of a response.

I grab my computer to "grade" and walk over with them.

"Why are you coming with us to the classroom next door again?" Anaia asks.

I have my answer rehearsed and ready to go in my arsenal.

"I have to grade some assignments and I forgot to bring a jacket. I can't sit in the icebox today."

Carter shivers, thinking about it. "You're right, your room is always a frozen tundra." Luckily, they accept my response without hesitation.

The pair walk into the classroom, introduce themselves to Riley who migrates over from his Smartboard.

Before they get started, I ask in the sweetest voice I can muster, "Hey, can I borrow your office to grade? My room is an icebox."

"Uh, yeah, sure," Riley huffs. He unlocks his office, and steps in front of me to push all the papers on his desk into a makeshift pile.

"Sorry, I like to spread out all my notes," he reasons. There are papers covering every inch of his desk in a haphazard assortment. A police vest hangs on his chair and clear storage bins line the corners. Supplies for his classes are all labeled on the front. Vests, crime scene tape, 3d printed guns, the works.

I walk over to his chair and settle in. As soon as he steps out and shuts the door. I flip open my laptop and click over to the grades tab, just in case. Thankfully, the curtains on his office windows are drawn, so no one can see what I'm up to. That would have been a non-starter if they had a clear sightline. Things to keep in mind for other missions. Making quick work I fish the key out of my pocket and bend down, quietly opening the middle cabinet. The filing cabinets are ancient, so it takes skill to jiggle the key without shaking the whole thing. I slide out the drawer, trying to keep the deep file cabinet groan to a minimum as files bob around like the cafeteria jello.

I drop the extra SD card in my pocket loose at the bottom of the cabinet in case I need insurance. I may be an amateur at this whole investigative business, but I'm never without a plan B. And they act like teaching skills aren't applicable to other things. After what feels like a few painful minutes of trying to decipher Riley's handwriting, I hit the jackpot and see Anders, organized by date instead of alpha by name, towards the back. I open the file and quickly snap what I hope aren't blurry photos of the autopsy report and double-sided witness list.

Moments after, I secure the files back in their wonky file system. Riley walks in as I'm still over the open cabinet. I give myself a silent pep talk, trying not to freak out about the fact that this whole situation is about to depend on the strength of my acting skills. Technically lying, but acting sounds better. I'm doing this to solve a murder. It's all for Mr. Anders.

"What the heck, Dannon?" He thunders with a pissed off glare that could make the most hardened criminal confess in seconds.

CHAPTER FOURTEEN

Cohen

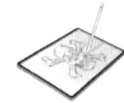

I'm strolling by with my copies for tomorrow when I see that someone put a tutu on Gerald, the training manikin, again. The seniors thought it would be a hilarious prank and moved him into my room. I almost jumped out of my skin when I turned on the light the next morning and found him sitting in my chair.

Papers in hand, I make a beeline for the open door to find two students packing up their camera equipment, not so stealthily trying to listen as they break everything down.

I go to stand behind Riley, but he's blind with fury, fists clenched at his sides and he doesn't even notice me.

Elle laughs awkwardly. "Oh sorry. You left your file cabinet open and when I walked by, the SD card in my pocket fell out."

She peers down, spots something, and is elbow deep in the cabinet before fishing out an SD card.

"Here it is. I don't have enough budget money to go around losing these." She smiles in mock relief.

This seems to diffuse the situation, as Riley lets out a deep exhale and his hands uncurl.

"Got it. I thought you were trying to look through my files, which would constitute the offense of burglary and tampering with physical and exculpatory evidence. Which are felonies by the way." He chuckles darkly. A pit in my stomach forms. Maybe we should've googled that before blindly deciding to break into Riley's files.

We join in the awkward chuckle chorus, and Riley notices me for the first time as Elle is shutting her laptop.

"Hey," I announce, feigning nonchalance.

"Just making copies when I heard something and came to check it out," I reason, holding up my papers for emphasis.

Riley just nods in response as Elle and I make a beeline out of the room, ready to be rid of his distrustful eyes on our backs as we exit.

I stroll with Elle casually as we step over the threshold of her classroom.

We are both in a state of stunned silence as the students clang around the equipment room unpacking their camera bags.

It's almost painful waiting for them to leave, so we can discuss what just happened.

For something to do, I set my copies at the end of her desk, and start pacing the room. I push in chairs and check the floor for trash, while Elle puts everything in her teacher bag. The students eye us suspiciously, no doubt having seen the Instagram account of doom and wondering why we're one of the few still here.

I finally felt like I was making progress in our relationship, only for some teenagers to freak E out with that account. They tell us goodnight and head home for the day.

I pick up the last scrap of trash, toss it in the trash can, and glance at Elle as we take a deep breath. She puts up a finger, signaling to me not to open the floodgates yet, and nods toward the studio. She unlocks the door, and we file inside.

"I share a wall with Riley, and I don't want to risk him hearing. The studio is soundproof," she says with an open arm gesture and a proud smile.

"That was wayyy too close." I spew, trying not to relive the terror in my chest when I thought Riley had caught Elle.

"I know, but luckily, I had Plan B already in place." She smiles maniacally.

"So you put an SD card in the file cabinet on purpose?" I question, starting to connect the dots.

"Yep, I figured if I got caught, I could pretend I was looking for it in the cabinet. That's a mentor tip. Always have a Plan B, because Plan A will go sideways at some point. Do you think he bought it?"

I sigh in relief. I would blame myself if Elle got caught on one of our missions. "I mean, you aren't in handcuffs right now, so I'd say it worked, but we need to tread lightly moving forward. What did you find?"

Demeanor shifting as if she didn't almost just get arrested, Elle happily taps on her phone. I can see the adrenaline rush leaving her body as her shoulders start to slowly sink down to their normal place.

"Look, I got the autopsy report and the witness list!" she exclaims, holding the phone too close to my face to read. I take it from her and start flipping through the pictures. "Woah, is that witness list two pages?"

She sighs. "Yeah, I never said we don't have a lot of work ahead of us."

"How are we going to get through all these suspects and work our full-time jobs?" I question, my voice raising an octave.

She gives me a reassuring look as if it's the simplest thing.

"We cross a name off the list one at a time. I'll text this to you and we can decide who we want to start with."

"Ok, but I already know who we should start with," I say decisively.

"Who?"

"Well, I'm assuming the two highlighted names are our top suspects. Mr. Joseph is one, who we already spoke to. And the only other name is Mr. Pat McPatterson. Who will have more insight into a PTA event than the president himself?"

"Ooh good point, He is going to be on campus Friday to set up for the Back 2 Cool carnival."

I scrunch my nose in mild disgust. "They're really running with the whole Back 2 Cool thing."

"Yep," she says, emphasizing the p with a pop.

"And they understand the irony of corny slogans at a high school where teenagers will mock them relentlessly?"

She smirks. "They do, but like a lot of things, you'll realize that Pat McPatterson doesn't care. He'll just do what he wants anyway," she states it as if it's an indisputable fact. Who gave Pat McPatterson control of the school? It's not like he's the principal. He's the PTA president sure, but that's a volunteer position. It doesn't hold any real power. Or does it?

I'm stumbling out of my car, drunk with exhaustion from a full day of teaching and investigating. I sling my teacher bag over my shoulder and start the trek to my 3rd floor apartment. The stairs are in sight as I notice the blond ponytail that I left 30 minutes ago making her way down the hall on the first floor.

"Elle?" I question, wondering how fast I can Google, *does sleep deprivation make you hallucinate*, when she whips around, her ponytail almost hitting her eye, but instead whipping her cheek, causing her to blink in further disorientation.

"Cohen?" She matches my incredulous expression.

We practically shout, "What're you doing here?" in unison.

"I'm just heading to my apartment." I point back towards the stairs.

"With your friend from college, Ren, right?"

"Yeah." I nod.

"Well, I was just going to my apartment." She points backward.

"With Jade." I shake my head in shock.

"Yep," she mutters.

I scratch my head. "So we've been living in the same unit a few floors apart this whole time?"

"I guess so."

A hint of a smile slowly spreads across my face, in spite of the sticky humidity that already claimed a few strands of hair that are clinging to the back of my neck.

"See, you're just closer to my bookcase. Now you have to see it."

She narrows her eyes. "Is that a euphemism, or..." she trails off.

I shrug, "It could be."

Elle scrunches her nose while her eyes narrow in irritation. I haven't seen that look from her in a while.

"I'm standing here trying to process this and you're making jokes again." She groans, but it seems more for show, than actual irritation. Am I growing on her? I try to tell myself not to get my hopes up, but the pang in my chest suggests I'm more invested than I thought.

"Wouldn't you rather have a joke, euphemism, or general humorous statement?" I offer.

Brows furrowed, she ventures, "As opposed to?"

"Two of us freaking out. You freak out enough for both of us. One of us has to reign it in," I say with a smile. Hopefully, she'll realize I'm just messing with her.

"Well, my students would boast about how calm, cool, and collected I am at all times," she finishes in mock offense. Her face cracks into a grin as she loses the battle to school her features.

Mid laugh, I wheeze, "See? You can't even pretend that's the truth."

This throws us into a fit of laughter. We're both fighting for breath, as a door adjacent to our impromptu gathering opens a crack, pauses a moment, then shuts loudly, sending a clear message.

I glance at the door and try to bring us back to reality.

"Before we get thrown out of our own complex, it's probably a good idea if we actually make it inside our apartments. See you tomorrow E."

"See you tomorrow, Cohen," she says with a wave.

I turn to go, the leftover laugh embers still bubbling out as I make my way back towards the staircase. I make it two steps before I turn over my shoulder, realizing I don't know which unit she's in, but I can see the general direction she's walking.

Maybe one day she'll actually let me in, I think, as I walk towards my unit. Will anything ever happen, or am I just setting myself up to get hurt with these delusional daydreams?

Chapter Fifteen

Elle

I f this were a movie, a montage would fill the screen set to an upbeat pop/rock song as we spend the next few weeks crossing off suspects on the list. It would be a mash up of clips of Cohen and I talking to parents, teachers, and admin alike, frustratingly adding gold stars to their pictures, clearing more suspects on the murder board, while spending countless hours in the welcoming cocoon of The Plot Thickens. Cohen was mainly getting the hang of the teaching thing, and I was hanging on. By this point in the school year, all things are starting to pick up steam and I'm just trying to keep up. Summer is long gone, the newness of the year has fully worn off, and we have a long way to go before fall and winter breaks.

On Monday students don't have to come to school, but like many of the perks of working at a school, the teachers do. We have a staff development day, which is a new kind of torture. Most development days are set to the tune of hours long presentations in what educators coin "sit and get" sessions, which are an ode back to college lectures, but on topics like classroom management, state testing, or whatever tactics are trending, given by a speaker who hasn't seen the inside of a classroom in at least ten years.

On the bright side, you can eat snacks, talk to your friends, and use the restroom whenever you want, but your brain is slowly frying like an egg on a frying pan, and you just want a nap. However, I think I would rather have my brain fried than the fresh torture disguised as fun that is a full day of team building activities. That's right. A. Full. Day.

Like any event you're dreading, it comes up faster than a student can turn on their Chromebook, and I try not to visibly scowl as Jade and I make our way to the gym. We always ride together on PD days.

She bumps my shoulder. "I don't know why you didn't ask Cohen to tag along, we have plenty of room in my car."

I groan. "Jade, drop it."

Undeterred, she continues, "I'm sorry, but he literally lives in our unit. If that's not fate trying to get you two to spend more time together, I don't know what is?"

I hum in agreement and change the subject. This leads to a detailed discussion about what shoes look best with straight leg jeans and Jade doesn't bring up Cohen again.

The lights of the gym are too ungodly bright for 8 in the morning. I squint, trying to muster up any enthusiasm. The speaker crackles, causing us all to jump as Ezra, our AP, grabs the microphone, treating us to an assault on our ears. He conveniently forgets to turn it off while grabbing hold of it and bringing it to his mouth.

"Happy Development Day, y'all. Before we get to the fun, this is a reminder to not allow students to go to the restroom with their backpacks or food of the Cheeto variety. I don't understand why students feel the need to waste a bag of Cheetos or how they came up with this idea, but this is the third time the upstairs toilets have been clogged, and we would like our janitors to make it until the end of the school year. Please and thank you."

He claps his hands together, in fake enthusiasm, making sure to slap the microphone in the process. "Today, we're going to start with a few warm-up relay games, and then you'll get to see the surprise we prepared for you in the courtyard."

Just when I think AP Ezra's monologue is complete, he comes back with one final blow, so close to turning off the mic, but pulling it back to his mouth at the last minute. In all the flailing, the feedback that fills the room is a sound that could make teenagers cry.

"Oh, I almost forgot. Go ahead and choose a partner. They will be with you the whole day through the relay games and a surprise activity. Choose wisely!"

I turn to Jade, about to laugh about being each other's partner, because duh, it's a given, only to find her walking away from me.

I reach out fruitlessly trying to grab her arm. "Hey, what are you doing, partner?"

"Sometimes fate just needs a little shove." She winks at me. *Traitor.*

"Go find your own partner." She nods in Cohen's general direction across the gym.

Thanks to her movement, I look that way and we make eye contact. Crap, now it would be awkward if I picked someone else. It's strictly a mentor/mentee thing.

I'm about halfway there as we make our way over to each other, when Layla blocks my view of Cohen. I'm close enough to hear their conversation, and I catch her asking to be his partner.

That's a lot of hair flipping for this early in the morning. I start slowly stepping backward, glancing around to find other available souls in an effort to save myself from further embarrassment. That is until I'm rooted in my spot at his words.

"I actually already have a partner, sorry," he says, nodding toward me.

She turns around to see me, and her face falls a bit.

"Right, see you around," Layla says, already searching for a replacement.

"You don't have to be my partner. You could have gone with her. Don't let me hold you back," I reason.

"Nope, I want you," he says with determined finality. *Uh, okay.* I'm sure he didn't mean it like that. I see a flicker of something, as he realizes what he actually said and tries to recover.

"I mean as my partner. For the day!" he clarifies with a small laugh, a flush creeps up his neck peeking out from his collar. We just stared at each other a bit too long for me to buy that, but I'm not about to go there, so I brush it off. This shouldn't make my stomach feel like I'm mid roller coaster, but it does.

Determined not to smile at him like an idiot, I respond, "Of course. Now, let's go win a relay."

I might have overestimated my athletic abilities and overall hand-eye coordination as we fumble the balloon for the fourth time.

Still wondering what thoughts were going through the assistant principals' heads as they planned our relay, Cohen and I are deadlocked in a staring contest through a balloon. His features are distorted in the green hue of the latex, which should make him look sickly or some alien hybrid, but unfortunately it doesn't. His look of concentration mirrors mine as we try to keep moving forward at a pace so slow, Mr. Joseph could pass us on the cleaning Zamboni. The goal of this game is to balance the balloon between our foreheads and walk to the tape and back.

Like all relay activities, you always start with a false sense of your general capabilities, only to realize halfway through that you are generally uncoordinated and should give up while you're ahead.

After the fifth balloon drop, we devise a plan.

"Ok, put your arms out, but bracket them by your sides," he instructs.

I do exactly that and his hands grip my elbows. This is substantially easier than our posture before where I kept smashing my face further into the balloon with every uneven step as we tried, but failed to match each other's pace.

With this newfound strategy, we pick up more of a real pace and coast to the finish. We pass the balloon to the next group, and I'm suddenly thankful we were the first pair to use it, because this feels like how diseases are spread, and make our way to the back of the line. When half the staff calls in for subs this week, no one should be surprised. We stand almost shoulder to shoulder, sporting matching exhausted smiles; the front of his hair is sticking straight up from static electricity, and I strongly resist the urge to fix it.

Jade would never let me live that down. Realizing that my hair is also probably living a life of its own, I fix it quickly before we turn to face each other.

"We make a great team," he points out.

"I think we already know that," I respond, referencing our sleuthing adventures.

"Three guesses for what our surprise is... GO!" I challenge, trying to quash what could have turned into a tender moment.

"Lesson plans for the next two weeks are due today, we have to wear business professional dress to school from now on, or I guess it could be a good thing. A lifetime supply of tissues?"

I giggle and respond with my own, "Ok, it's dodgeball against the admin, time in our classrooms, or we're cleaning up the Cheeto mess to give the janitors a break?"

At the last suggestion, he barks out a loud laugh that has everyone in front of us craning their necks back to give us a mix of unamused, skeptical looks. Except for a few of the women in front of us, who are silently awing us. Crap, now no one will ever believe that the dating rumors aren't true.

Whoops sound off at the front of our line in celebration, distracting everyone from our display. I could psychoanalyze why that doesn't bother me as much as it should, but for now, I'm too busy clapping because our line actually won. Maybe this team building day won't be so bad after all?

CHAPTER SIXTEEN

Cohen

"This is a cumulation of my nightmares, why did I think this day was looking up?" Elle mutters.

Intrigued, I inquire, "Why, what's so bad about it?"

She stares up at the stacked piles of hay, artfully extending in all directions. "For starters, from our vantage point we can't see the end of this monstrosity, so we have no idea what we're in for. Then, we'll get stuck, and what if we can't get out? Will they just assume everyone's done at a certain point and we'll have to spend the night sleeping on the ground until they start taking it down?"

I'm trying not to crack a smile during this entire, very dramatic monologue, but her hands are flailing and she's working herself up in the cutest way possible. But, because I know we don't share the same feelings and we're in front of our colleagues, I tell myself to remain neutral. Or at least I don't think we feel the same way? Lately, I can't tell.

"Would it make you feel better if I told you I was a corn/hay maze champion?" I offer.

Her head jerks back in skepticism. "It would if that was a thing that existed."

I smirk. "I've done one of these at least once a year in Texas growing up, so I'm deserving of this self-appointed distinction."

"Well, here in Arkansas, hay mazes aren't a pinnacle of the fall season, unless you're five and at a pumpkin patch," she huffs defiantly.

Unable to leave it alone, I ruffle her hair just to mess with her a bit more. "Touché. Come on, we're wasting daylight if we want to make it out before nightfall. We only have 6-7 hours max until it gets dark." I motion for her to follow my lead.

"Did Ezra say we could switch partners?" she questions, scanning the pairings before begrudgingly following me to the start of the maze.

The bright side of this whole maze excursion besides getting to spend time with E is that the APs said we could go home early once we come out the other side, providing me with extra motivation to get us out in record time. Impressing Elle with my corn maze expertise wouldn't hurt either. We could use that time to get something done at The Plot Thickens, or maybe I could somehow convince her of a date-ish situation if I use the correct phrasing.

I turn my focus to the seemingly endless hay bales stretched out in front of us. I may have exaggerated a bit when I called myself a corn/hay maze champion, but I was used to small hay mazes with my cousins or corn mazes where you could still see the sun peaking through the tops, reminding you of the world outside the maze. This was something else entirely.

Bales stacked up prevented shortcut seekers from bulldozing their way through, and they were high enough that you would have to look up to confirm sunlight still exists.

Straight ahead is the golden tan hue that never seems to end. I try to gather my thoughts, burdened by the need to be the calm one in this partnership. Weaving in and out of the easiest sections of the maze, we try to keep our pace up. "You know, maybe I've been listening to too many true crime podcasts, but this maze would be the perfect backdrop for a murder."

Not expecting this angle, curiosity gets the best of me. "Why?"

"Because it's secluded, the entire staff is running around, so it would be impossible to solve, they'll literally clean up the crime scene for you, and…"

I cut her off, "Ok, that's all a bit too logical for me. Tell me about this when we're out of the murder maze, please."

"That's fine, not everyone's cut out for this kind of stuff." She smiles as if the roles weren't reversed five minutes ago.

I huff out a laugh at the irony of her statement and we're both momentarily distracted from our worries. We walk in silence for a few minutes, as she lets me take the lead. All that can be heard is the distant chatter of the other groups perpetually ahead of us, and the steady crunch of our shoes flattening the grass and hay mixture blanketing the once empty courtyard.

Eyes trained to the ground, I notice a dollar bill caked with dirt. It probably fell out of another teacher's pocket. Something about it looks off, but I can't put my finger on it, so I force my eyes up to focus on the task at hand.

I'm getting distracted by anything at this point in an attempt to forget the humidity that gathers in every forced breath and causing the hairs to cling to the nape of my neck. Even though it's probably been 30 minutes, it feels like hours, and the chatter has lessened, leading me to believe several groups are already done.

Similar to bikers on a hiking trail, I hear the "On your left," before I can register a group pounding through the maze as if something is chasing them.

Instinct kicking in, I don't have time to second guess as I place my palms on E's shoulders and pull her out of the way. An electric current hits my system and I faintly hear an "ow" from her end right before our shoulders slam against the sharp, unforgiving pieces of hay sticking out from the bale. Even though we basically body slam the bales, they don't budge. I guess plan B to move the bales aside to get out of the maze isn't as viable of an option as I previously thought. Senses alight, I'm scanning behind us to make sure nothing will pop out and start chasing us too.

But there's nothing. And no one, just us. We're both rubbing our shoulders and trying to calm ourselves after that jarring assault on our senses.

"I can't decide which hurt worse. When you shocked me, or the body check we gave the hay bale," she declares.

Before I have time to answer, she continues, "Seriously, you're not even wearing anything that would store static electricity. How is that possible?"

I'm convinced this is another kind of electricity, but I might as well go along with it. We're both lost in thought but seem to come to the same conclusion simultaneously as we shout at each other, "The balloons!"

"Wait, is that even possible this long after the relay?" I question.

"I don't know, ask the science teachers," she suggests.

"When we get out of the maze," I supply.

"The murder maze." She sighs in agreement.

"Do we have to call it that?" I whine.

"When you have a better name, we can call it that," she challenges.

"Yeah, yeah whatever." I smile.

"Well, you're the master name creator. Any ideas on our catch-phrase yet?"

"I don't need your negativity today. Let's just focus on the maze," I suggest with a huff of laughter, disguised as frustration.

She looks over at my hands, which are still on both of her arms. I'm about to move them when I notice a lone strand of hay sitting in her golden hair. I pluck it and release my grip on her wordlessly.

Elle seems too stunned to speak, so we just stare at each other dumbfounded for a bit, until she breaks eye contact and trudges on ahead. She doesn't know that I'm still planted in the spot, and I notice her hand fly up to her chest, as her shoulders rise and fall from a steadying breath.

I smile to myself at the confirmation that maybe my feelings aren't as one sided as I was previously convinced. Even though this would be the perfect time to throw a *Breakfast Club* worthy fist in the air, we have a murder maze to get out of. Ugh, we really need to stop calling it that.

After finally coming out the other side of the maze, we're filled with relief. The rest of our journey passed by in a blur, as we trial and error our way out, feet heavy and minds numb from the constant puzzle solving. I will never make fun of my mom for her crossword puzzle obsession after this.

Puzzles are more work than I thought. I'm about to pull E into a totally normal, we just escaped a hay maze hug, when I spot someone ahead. The sun casting them as a silhouetted figure.

I can't tell if the figure in front of me is a mirage of my own making, or conveniently here. I feel a tap at my shoulder as E nods towards Pat McPatterson, alerting me to the reality of our luck. We had already strategized on how to talk to him since our normal, albeit amateur tactics, wouldn't work on him.

"Hey, Pat, right?" I start. We agreed I should take the lead on this one.

"Cohen, how's year one?" he asks.

"Uh, I'm surviving it," I answer honestly. I didn't realize he even knew who I was.

"How's the PTA?" I supply weakly.

"Fantastic!" He booms, clapping his hands together. "We're in the midst of the Halloween Carnival and finalizing the application process for this year's Scholars of Tomorrow scholarship," he says with a megawatt smile. It seems over the top for a casual conversation, but I'm learning he's pretty intense no matter the situation.

Trying to ease my way in, I continue the small talk train I seem to have boarded.

"E— I mean Elle, was telling me about that." I motion to her.

Preening, he responds, "Mrs. Dannon helped a lot with several of the events that made the scholarship possible. We couldn't have done it without help from the teachers and donors' support. And now, our first recipient is at school, completely covered for the next four years." She smiles graciously at his comment.

Treading lightly, I start, "Speaking of PTA events, the carnival will be the first since the Back 2 Cool Night incident, right?"

Pat's smile immediately vanishes, and he glances down at his shoes for a moment, and when he looks up, his eyes are glassy. "Yes, Mr. Anders will never be forgotten. It's heartbreaking how a freak allergy flare up can lead to fatality, so quickly."

I'm about to correct him when E jumps in, practically vibrating with unanswered questions.

"Did you see —it happen?" She whispers the last two words.

He shrugs, seemingly unbothered. "No, I was in the auditorium in the sound booth. The mic kept shorting out, so they needed someone to monitor."

A sense of pride wells in my chest as I realize we can cross off another name on the murder board and stick one of our now trademark gold star stickers by Pat McPatterson's name. It's funny how we had worked ourselves up into believing it had to be him, but an alibi doesn't lie.

It feels like we're actually making progress in the investigation.

Elle and I walk back towards the parking lot, relief from escaping the maze evident in our smiles.

Elle's smile fades, and she walks closer to me, so our shoulders bump. Lowering her voice she says, "We need to confirm McPatterson's alibi. I get a weird feeling from him."

"How are we going to confirm?" I press. Clearly, she isn't ready to mark him off just yet.

"I'll ask one of my students who works the booth at all events. He's in tech theatre, so he always helps out at that stuff," she reasons. Our fingers brush for a split second, before she puts more distance between us.

CHAPTER SEVENTEEN

Elle

We are trying to stay ignorant of a certain Instagram account, but that doesn't mean it isn't in full swing and gaining followers fast. It's giving us the constant uneasy feeling that we're being watched. To cope, we escape to The Plot Thickens most days after school. By now, the bookstore employees know us on a first name basis. I wave at my favorite barista as I walk in and sit down in our spot. Cohen's already seated, and smiles when we make eye contact. That shirt really brings out his eyes. *Focus on the investigation. Not him.*

"You know what's bugging me?" Cohen laments.

"Is this a guessing game or is that a rhetorical question? Because I have a few theories," I confess.

"Ok, now I want to hear." He leans closer, giving me a subtle nod. "Go ahead."

"Hmmm. Is it the number of students that tried to submit late work today on the last day of the quarter, or the fact that Halloween is getting closer, and they haven't decorated the school, oooor I got it!

You don't want to work at the haunted house at the Eerie Extravaganza thing at the school?"

"Why can't they come up with one cool name? It's almost painful at this point." Cohen lets out a humorless laugh.

I pull up the murder board. "Agreed, but you'll get used to it. Wait, did I guess correctly?"

"No, you just sent me off a tangent. What's actually bugging me is Mr. Joseph," he huffs.

"Ok, I'm not following. Did the spray cleaner he uses on the iMacs leave streaks again?" I ask.

"Unfortunately, that's a given. I still get the feeling he's hiding something, and we need to figure out what it is." He clicks with more force, taking out his frustration on his laptop.

"True, but what can we do?" I wonder. I add a star beside Pat's picture, his pink polo practically popping off the page. "We can cross Pat off the list. My student cleared him. He was barking orders at everyone all night." We high five at the small win. Another day, another suspect off the list.

"So, what do you want to do about Mr. Joseph? He clearly doesn't want to tell us anything." I sigh, exasperated.

"According to my extensive research—" Cohen starts.

"Of watching TV," I finish for him.

"Of watching TV," he concedes with a good-natured smirk before continuing.

"We have two options, we can call his bluff and pretend we already know OR, we can go full bad cop and accuse him of something and see if he gives us a clue," Cohen suggests.

I take a minute to process, considering the implications of both options. *Dang it.* Cohen is the only person on the planet that could watch detective shows and actually gain something practical. I'm not about to let him know that, though.

"I say we call his bluff. If we went full bad cop on him, then our iMacs would be extra streaky, and gum might 'accidentally' be left under the desks. Let's not mess with one of the few colleagues that makes our lives easier."

"Good point, I can't get all that gum myself," he agrees.

"Call his bluff it is," I say with the pep in my step that only forms when an item is checked off my to-do list, or we make forward progress. The TV shows don't depict the monotonous frustration that comes with grueling research and chasing leads that turn up nothing over and over again.

I glance at the bookstore employee arranging a display of new re-leases. Tearing my eyes away from temptation, I stand up from my chair in our usual spot at the back of the store.

"Ok, let's go. I'm sure Bookstore Barb wants to get home to her family sometime in this millennium."

Cohen lets out a laugh and glances my way. "Bookstore Barb?"

"Yeah, it's how I remember names. I assign them some kind of qualifier that tells me something about their location, appearance, or relationship to me."

"What's my qualifier?" Cohen instantly asks.

Oh crap. I didn't think he'd go there. I can't, under any circum-stances, tell him he was Captivating Cohen. After the moment we ran into each other, it's the only thing that popped into my head and clouded any other qualifier ever being an option. I'm definitely not telling him that, though. It's very PG, but still, I don't want to give him any ideas. I don't feel ready to show my cards just yet. I'm racking my brain, trying to think of something to use in its place.

"Cautious Cohen," I mumble, thankful for my teaching brain that's skilled at thinking on the spot. This seems like a bland alternative to the actual thing, but I'll go with it.

His face falls a bit, and he looks surprised. "Why cautious?"

Stalling for time, I look down at my feet and take a beat. "It's purely from when we met. You opened your door to see what was going on and we made eye contact, remember?"

A flush rises on my cheeks as I slowly look up to meet his gaze, which is locked on me. "Yeah, I remember."

"Well, the only word I could use to describe the look on your face was cautious. And you still joined our crazy group anyway, so it all worked out," I finish, done with this conversation.

"Ok, but now that you know me, I want a new qualifier," he insists.

I sputter, "What? It doesn't work like that."

"Why not?" He runs a hand through his hair.

"Now that I know you, I don't need a qualifier. You're Cohen. I'm not going to forget who you are."

He smiles softly. "I hear you, but there are so many other options. Like Compelling Cohen, Cute Cohen, Confident Cohen, or my personal favorite, Charismatic Cohen." His smile transforms into a full on smirk as he tries to reason with me.

"Your answer tells me you heard me but didn't listen. I. Don't. Need. A. Qualifier." I articulate.

"Just because you don't need something, doesn't mean you don't want it," Cohen retorts.

Yeah, this doesn't seem like it's just about the naming thing anymore. Before my brain can process a response, I let out a bit of truth that seems a touch too vulnerable.

"I never said I didn't want it," I practically whisper, afraid to say the words in full volume for fear that it will cement them into reality. This doesn't stop him from hearing me.

"You say one thing, but your body language gave you away. I don't know why you can't tell me yet, but when you're ready, I'm here."

We both stare at each other wordlessly a beat too long, until the sound of the crosswalk mechanically shouting, "Walk now," acts as a bucket of water, catapulting us back into real life. The contrast of the quiet of five seconds ago with the cars, wind, chatter, and shop bells ringing is jarring, as if a TV that was on mute, suddenly got turned up to full volume. We both continue to the parking lot across the street, almost shoulder to shoulder. I can practically hear him thinking, and I can't figure out where to take our conversation from here.

I have to do something, because the silence apart from the pounding of our feet on pavement and subtle swish from the fabric of our pant legs rubbing together as we stride in unison is about to break me.

"What are your plans for the rest of the day?" Is the first thing that springs from my lips. So much for playing it cool.

Cohen glances at me out of his peripherals, eyebrows raised, as if he didn't notice the silence the same way I did. Going with the jarring change of subject, he answers my question.

"I still have a few things to do for this week's lesson plans, so I'm sure that will take pretty much the rest of the day. What about you?"

"Same, I have a few small things to do. Then I'll probably read until Jade makes me put my book down and hang out with her."

He sucks in a breath of laughter. "When did our lives get this exciting?"

I smile. "We're teachers, as soon as they gave us a badge, it became a job and personality all in one during the school year."

A worried spark flashes behind his irises. "So, you're telling me it doesn't get better?"

"Which part?" I bite my lip, telling myself I won't lie.

"Everything."

I pause for a moment, trying to figure out how to accurately describe it. "It does get better. But I'm on year four and I finally feel like I know what I'm doing. That doesn't mean I don't still plan things, adjust and grow, it's just in a different way."

He nods, placated by this response on the surface, but his fingers drum against his thigh in silent indignation.

We get to our respective cars, say our goodbyes, and I can't decide if our crosswalk conversation has been forgotten or tabled? We fall back into our normal cadence. Leaving me to wonder if it's by design or a lack of us knowing how to move forward.

I can't leave this be, which is why I go to my own personal Dear Abby. Which is how I find myself currently sitting cross legged on our gray couch surrounded by the assortment of colorful throw pillows, staring down at Jade, who is on the floor painting her toes.

The polish bottle is teetering on a groove in the carpet, and it's taking everything in me not to right it. At least if it gets on the rug, it'll blend into the pattern and will hardly be noticeable. Jade paints in a steady rhythm as she digests the saga.

"You know what you have to do, right?" she muses.

"If I did, I wouldn't be asking you," I reason, playing with the fringe of the throw pillow in my lap.

"You would have filled me in either way, so chill." She stops mid stroke, pointing the nail polish wand in my direction before continuing. "You have to make a move."

I sputter, "What? Why? What if he doesn't reciprocate?"

"Ok, let's take a step back. Tell me if I'm right."

"I think you think you're right either way, so what does—"

She shoots me a glance that stops my train of thought. The quiet hum of the A/C is the soundtrack of the moment as she stares at me a second longer.

"Cohen agreed to be the other half of your crime solving duo when he saw you were upset, gives up his free time working with you at your favorite bookstore, talks to you in the hallway between every class period, and hangs on every word you say." She sighs. "Meanwhile, I can't even get anyone to text me back. Including my own boyfriend. He says he's just busy with basketball, but he's always busy with basketball and I'm starting to think it's me. But we'll talk about that later."

Jade levels me with a tired look. "Elle-Belle, he likes you. A lot. He shows you every day. My guess is that he can't tell if you feel the same and doesn't want to freak you out. Which is so self-aware and sweet, ugh. You've got to make a move," she declares.

"Well, that's vague," I answer, frustrated by the endless options of what this "move" could be.

"If I gave you an answer, then it wouldn't be from you."

I nod, knowing she's right. Now to put myself on the endless rollercoaster that will involve coming up with ideas, only to veto them until I find the perfect solution. While teaching and trying to solve this case.

CHAPTER EIGHTEEN

Cohen

I'm minding my own business, when something hard and plastic hits my arm and bounces off with a pop, echoing as it shatters to the floor with a hard crash as pieces scatter on the faux hard wood floor. I stare at the object, halted in my tracks as I take in the remote sprawled out back, cover ajar, and batteries spilled out on the floor.

"What the—"I start.

"Can you just chill? I'm sure you'll ace whatever test you have to take, or lesson you have to teach. Scuffing our floors with your pacing won't help anyone." Ren chides, trying and failing to provide comfort from his perch on the couch.

"You threw the remote at me?" I answer in disbelief.

"Yeah, sorry. I called your name and got nothing. Drastic measures were needed," he says in his signature flat tone that sounds anything but empathetic.

Normally, Ren's naturally calm demeanor is comforting when I'm upset, but today it's getting on my nerves. Along with everything else.

There's an unshakeable annoyance stirring in my bones, and swirling in my gut, causing me to fight against the urge to lash out at Ren. It won't do anything to solve my current predicament.

"Are you going to tell me what's eating you or brood all night?" Ren gives a pointed look in my direction.

"I don't want to talk about it," I grumble.

"Wow, we're gonna play it that way. Fine. I'm not going to ask again. You're not my girlfriend. I don't have to coax anything out of you," he huffs.

Whether it's the reverse psychology of it all, or the need to get this off my chest, I give in almost instantly.

"Elle and I were at the bookshop and we were talking about school related things that turned not so school related, and we kind of had a moment, but then went back to normal. I can't tell if she reciprocates my feelings and I don't know where to go from here," I huff in a heap of frustrated chaos.

Ren blinks in response, taken aback by my mini outburst. He tilts his head slightly and narrows his eyes, taking a beat to process. "Ok." He continues nodding. "Ok."

"If you say ok one more time," I say, glaring at his smirk.

Looking me right in the eye, he continues, "Oookay. So, you didn't actually say 'I like you' or 'I want to go on a date,' did you?"

"Not in so many words," I admit sheepishly.

"That would be a no. Have you ever considered that she may be feeling as confused as you are and unsure if you want to be with her?" His tone is measured and contemplative.

"I flirt with her all the time." I scoff, not understanding how he can be so dense.

He laughs. "Sure, but flirting is the lowest form of commitment. It just means you think she's cute. You two are co-workers and it would be awkward if one of you had unrequited feelings for the other. Maybe she can't tell if you're serious about dating."

Crap. *Why is Ren always the voice of reason?*

"True. But what can I do to show her I'm serious?" I question, feeling like I'm trying to grade a test without an answer key.

"Do something cool you think she'll like," he says, gaze drifting back to the muted TV, already losing interest.

"Thanks for being as vague as humanly possible," I complain.

"Well, I don't know her. Think of what her ideal date would be, and do that."

He pauses, thinking for a moment.

"Then, take a piece of that perfect date and use it to ask her out."

"I was following you until I wasn't. Explain?" I question, wondering why this feels more like advanced calculus.

"Ok, so let's say her ideal date is watching the sunrise with coffee."

I laugh, shocked by his romantic answer.

"Don't say it. I know my example isn't top notch, but you get the idea. So, like I was saying, if that's her ideal date, then ask her out by writing something on the side of her coffee cup that you bring one morning. That way it reflects her preferences and makes her feel like you know her."

Ren sighs.

"That's all you're getting out of me, so take it or leave it." He proceeds to unmute the TV before I have a chance to answer, signaling the end of this heart to heart.

Long after I trudge back to my room, Ren's advice is still circling my thoughts.

Just as I feel something taking place, I hear the opening bars of the Jaws theme song. Sure enough, I look down and see "Mom" on screen.

Once I go to the next family dinner, I'll change her ringtone back to normal, but for now, it stays.

"Hey, Mom," I say, bracing myself.

"Cohen, is that you?" she asks dramatically.

"Yes, Mom. You called me."

She giggles, "You're right. Ya know, I just forgot what your voice sounds like."

Her frustration grows as she continues, "Son, you bale on your brother, and you still haven't been to a family dinner since summer. Pretty soon your seat will be taken by one of your siblings significant others."

"But none of them have been to a family dinner yet," I point out.

"I'm manifesting."

"Hey Mom. I don't mean to cut this short, but I have to finish up a couple things for school. I promise, I'll get to a dinner as soon as I can."

"Just don't forget about your family. We love you and miss you. We want to take advantage of everyone being in the same state before everyone goes off and gets married."

She is really pushing the marriage thing.

"I get it. Love you, Mom."

"Love you, son."

Once we hang up, I try to get my thoughts back on track. I think back to our interactions and the gesture crystalizes in front of me. I can't believe I didn't think of it before. Watch out, Elle Dannon. Prepare to be blown away.

CHAPTER NINETEEN

Elle

I spot Cohen and that familiar nauseous wave passes over me. This crush is getting to me. Yes, I'm calling it what it is, a crush. Between the literal static electricity in the hay maze (*I'm sticking to that story*), our conversation at the bookstore, and a cumulation of a million other small moments, I can't force myself in a different direction. Jade convinced me to make a "move," whatever that actually means. In true me fashion, I'm panicking, because it seems like the cons are too great. I think we already know I've made a pro-con list.

If anything happens with us, we'll have to work together. Or what if I've been reading this all wrong? What if I think the crosswalk is signaling me to step forward, only to be hit by oncoming traffic?

How mortifying would it be to be rejected by the one person I see as much as my students. At the end of the day, he's my classroom neighbor, mentee, and lives in my apartment building, rendering him utterly unavoidable. And the only thing more terrifying than actually falling for Cohen, is starting something, finding red flags, or worse, not having feelings, and our once fulfilling friendship turning stale and hollow.

I hate to admit that he not only makes me better, but his first-year teacher optimism keeps me going in what would otherwise be a hard year. The only life preserver I can toss myself is the disinterest I can fake to keep us in the in-between, instead of the aftermath of whatever a relationship would inevitably lead to.

This internal monologue is on repeat, as I see Cohen walk down the hall towards our rooms, and by default, me. Being the chicken I am, I decide to duck him for the moment, giving him a small wave, rushing into my room. I know I'll have to converse with him when we take another crack at Mr. Joseph while he's cleaning one of our rooms after school, but I need more time to collect myself. Having a crush as an adult is exhausting.

This seems like mental energy I'd rather put toward something else, but I know that isn't going to happen whether I want it to or not. The more I try to expel all Cohen related thoughts, the more they cloud my brain with a vengeance.

After what feels like a day of one thing after another, I'm finally making my way to Cohen's room. It's almost the week of Halloween and the carnival we have to work, so the kids are acting as if they've demolished a trick or treat pail of candy and declared free time all day every day. If I have to hear one more groan when confirming we have to work instead of watching a movie, I am going to lose it.

"Ready?" I ask as I poke my head through the door.

Cohen looks over at me from his comically small desk, miming putting on a detective badge, a smile igniting his features, making his hazel eyes shimmer with their signature green flecks. Pay attention to the task at hand. Cracking Mr. Joseph and moving forward with this case is the goal.

Having been momentarily distracted, a rush of guilt hits me as I think of all the things Mr. Anders won't be able to do now and all the moments he'll miss with his son. That's enough to get me back on track as I laugh at Cohen's cheesiness in spite of myself.

"Bad cop, reporting for duty," he adds to really solidify the cheese.

"You've got to get better material." I smirk.

"No time like the present," he says, standing up from his chair.

"And remember, we're calling his bluff, not going full bad cop," I remind him.

"Yeah, yeah, I remember. Nervous?" He bumps my shoulder, trying to search my face for a sign.

"I'm freaking out right now," I confess.

"Me too," he agrees with a shy smile.

"Well, you don't seem like it," I chide.

"I thought we already covered this. Weren't you the one that told me I mask everything with humor?" He lets out a self-deprecating laugh.

"Yeah, but if we're calling that humor, you really do need better material," I retort.

He guffaws in surprise. His eyebrow quirks at the exact moment he realizes I'm prolonging our exchange to procrastinate the interrogation looming over us. Wordlessly, he grabs my arm and drags me out his door. Even though it's only a few steps before his arm drops back to his side, I feel like I've been electrocuted. All the romance novels I've been reading really made this seem cuter than it really is, but I don't have time for this mid investigation.

Focus, I tell myself as I tune into the task at hand stepping under my door garland. Yes, I have a homemade garland of ribbons that took me all summer to painstakingly craft, hanging above the door via tension rod.

And yes, my taller students hate getting a face full of ribbon, but in my defense, it sets the cozy tone from the minute you step in. We crane our necks to see an unsuspecting Mr. Joseph unplugging his vacuum and moving onto the next step on his checklist.

I take a quiet breath and get ready to start the cadence Cohen and I practiced, when he notices us, eyeing us suspiciously. I don't know if my teacher skills take over my brain, or I just enjoy throwing our plan out the window, but I feel the need to adapt to the situation.

"Heyyyy, Mr. Joseph," I call out in a sing-song voice that doesn't quite have the finesse I was going for.

Either way, it works. Sort of. His shoulders relax a bit as he smiles at us, assuming we're not here to interrogate him again. The half smile that remains on my face slowly fades as I level the custodian with a look.

"Mr. Joseph, we know about the Back 2 Cool event," I say with mock confidence.

Cohen, ever the partner in crime, joins in, "And we don't want to tell Principal Mitchell, but we will," he squints and tilts his head forward just a bit, "for the kids' safety."

Now I know how the camera crew on Saturday Night Live feels, as I desperately try to stifle a laugh. I guess if the admin can guilt us with the "for the kids'" excuse, we can use it too.

We both use one of the key tenets of interviewing I taught Cohen earlier. We stare at him, without talking. As predicted, he starts rambling to fill the silence.

"You're not really gonna do that..." he stammers, twisting the cleaning cloth in his hands.

"Oh," I start—

"We are," Cohen finishes.

"Unless..." I say.

"You tell us more about what you saw," Cohen insists.

We both steal a glance at each other, unable to help sharing a smirk at our perfect synchronization.

"Fine, I saw her." Mr. Joseph confesses in a rush of words.

"Herrrr?" We both screech, taken aback.

CHAPTER TWENTY

Cohen

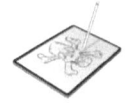

"Wait, back up..." I say in astonishment. "So you saw the killer, a woman?"

"Who is it?" E exclaims.

Mr. Joseph won't look at us, his eyes burning a hole in the carpet. "I didn't see her, exactly. Just her shoes."

Before I have time to follow up, E is already on it. "What did the shoes look like? Style? Color? Anything?" I can tell she'll keep hurling questions at him, so I place a reassuring hand on her shoulder and squeeze. She gets the message, giving him time to respond.

The custodian gives us the first real piece of evidence since we started this thing. "They were white sneakers. Like fancy sneakers, with those pinky gold stripes."

E holds up her lanyard. "Did it look like this color?"

Mr. Joesph glances at it, and his eyes light up. "Yes, just like that."

"Rose gold, got it," E mutters under her breath.

I don't know how rose gold is different from regular gold, but it seems like an important distinction that I'll inquire about later.

Curiosity gets the best of me and I ask, "Why didn't you tell someone about this earlier? Admin, Riley, anyone?"

He sighs, "It was such a whirlwind that night and I didn't realize that man died from the food until later. When I realized I saw something, I didn't come forward because the killer might come for me next," He gulps.

E's face softens, "Of course, that makes sense. When we pass this onto the police, we'll try to keep you anonymous." I elbow her knowing she can't guarantee a promise like that. Once we tell Riley, we'll have to disclose that information. She shrugs back at me with wide eyes. She doesn't know how to walk it back.

I offer a middle ground. "We'll try our best, but we can't make any promises. But, we won't offer your name up unless Riley specifically asks for it." Elle and I share a look, both confident Riley will ask.

However, this seems to placate Mr. Joseph, and we say our goodbyes, making our way back to my room to discuss. I plop into my desk chair, sending it on a one-way track to sink as close to the ground as possible. I pump the lever to put it back to a respectable height, adding it to my mental punch list of things to fix in my classroom.

"Are we really going to pass this onto Riley?" I question. I smile to myself, noticing E fixing a rogue piece of paper starting to peel away from my bulletin board.

She sighs, glancing back. "If we don't, we're withholding information and hindering the investigation, right?"

"According to Law and Order, you're correct. Just for the record, he wouldn't return the favor and give us information, so why should we help him?" I ask defiantly.

"I get that. But all he'd have to do is talk to Mr. Joseph and he'd know that we already talked to him."

"Fine, we'll do it your way," I concede.

"Will you do it with me? I don't think Riley's my biggest fan."

"Always," I say.

She smiles and looks at me a beat too long before reaching for her teacher bags. Wordlessly, I gently tug at one of the bags until she surrenders her grip and grab my own, my shoulder sagging with the weight of multiple bags. I can't believe she carries these every day, they're heavy. I subtly try to glance inside, when I feel the back of her hand lightly tap my bicep.

"You can carry my bags, but I draw the line at peeking inside," she chides with a smile.

I laugh. "Too late, E. I already saw and I have questions. Why do you have a bag full of mice?"

I should clarify they are of the computer variety and aren't at risk of crawling out of the bag.

"I didn't want you to think I'm weird, but I guess that ship has already sailed. All the mice in that bag are jammed, from the kids clicking too hard. I can fix them, but I would rather do it in front of the tv at home than in my classroom. I'll bring them back tomorrow ready to go," she explains.

"Are you out of budget money already?" I tease.

"No," she shrugs, "but I want to be a good steward of our resources, and it'll just take a little time to get them back."

"Your time. Non-contract time," I remind her.

"What's one more sacrifice?" she says, voice teetering on a fine line between joke and truth.

I have a sudden mental image of her, a forlorn look on her face, with a pile of computer mice spread out on the couch, rubbing her eyes with her sleeve, and barely watching what's on TV. I can't in good conscience give her this bag back without an offer of help.

I doubt this is what Ren had in mind when we were discussing the move I should make, but it's an excuse for us to see each other more outside of work in addition to our time at The Plot Thickens.

"Want help?" I offer.

Her face twists as if she's about to say no, and I swear I see something flash in her eyes before giving me an answer.

"Is this an excuse to see my apartment?" she asks, eyes narrowing.

"This was all for help, but if an unexpected benefit comes out of this, who am I to complain?" I say, feigning more confidence than I feel.

"You know what? Deal. I'm exhausted, and doing this alone would've taken me forever," she confesses.

"What wore you out today? Besides the normal teaching drain?" I ask.

"Besides them acting wild because it's Halloween next week? I have a student who has some stuff going on at home and she's been extra needy. Constantly asking me for my opinion on things just so I'll come over and chat." She looks down guiltily sighing. "Which is fine of course, but everyone else needs help too, and I feel like I don't have time to give everyone what they need before the period's over, which is leaving me frazzled and exhausted."

Understanding clouds my face as I take a beat before starting. "I know it might feel that way, but I just remember what my mom says."

"Which is?" she asks, eyes wide in anticipation.

"Whatever you're doing is always enough." We keep walking down the hall towards the parking lot in tandem pace as I continue. "When anyone needs something from you, they really just need you, so as long as you show up, you're doing enough."

I can see some of the guilt that has been weighing on her shoulders lift as she lets out a deep breath. Before I know it, we're getting in our cars and heading back to our apartment complex. You can't see it in the dark, but the mountainous landscape of Fayetteville is in full show this time of year. On the way to school, it feels like it belongs on a very aesthetic fall themed "For You" page. The technicolor hues of red, orange, and yellow melt together against the dewy, gray mornings, complete with fog hovering ominously above the mountaintops.

Now, the only view available is the murky dark, with a few hazy streetlights in the distance as we veer further away from the school and closer to our building. Two parking spots are available right next to each other, the single streetlamp overhead acting as a beacon. It's practically unheard of in the complex, which always seems to have more cars to park than spots open. Once in our spots, we match each other's look of astonishment, as I grab our bags from my car.

I know the general direction, but once we reach the hallway, I'm hyper aware of her cues, and still almost plow into her back as she stops short and opens the door. I put my hands on her shoulders in an attempt to catch my balance, and she quickly steps inside the door, torpedoing us inside.

Once we both catch our balance, she takes a step to the side so I can get a clear view. It's the exact opposite layout of our apartment. The living room backs up to the kitchen in the same open concept layout common in most colleges, or in our case, standard poor adult apartments. I try not to let my mouth hang open. Jade and Elle have transformed the place to look cozier than I thought possible. The overhead light is an antique that casts a soft yellow glow, washing the room in warmth.

Colorful pillows line the couch, which seems to be a requirement in any female inhabited space, and the TV is on top of an old trunk.

The kitchen is even cooler, with a gray brick backsplash and copper range hood.

"Did you do this all yourselves?" I ask in bewilderment.

She follows my sightline to the kitchen and laughs. "Jade was on an HGTV kick, the backsplash and copper are all peel and stick."

While I'm busy inspecting the backsplash, she pulls out a paper clip that's been pulled and flattened on the end with the curvy, rounded side still intact for easy grip and plops onto the couch. She moves pillows to the floor to make room for me to sit.

I immediately start laughing. "What do you need that shiv for, Prison Break?"

"What?! This is not a..." she trails off as she inspects it while her smile slowly transforms into a frown. "This is a shiv. Well, it's the only thing that will fix these," she says as she demonstrates how to fix the mouse using the makeshift tool. She sets about making me a matching shiv, and I just shake my head in disbelief that one person can have such a variety of talents. It must be a teacher thing. We're so used to having to make things work and troubleshoot any problem, that the veterans can fix a mouse with a paperclip shiv.

Glancing at her profile while trying not to stare, I add, "If we had a metal detector, you'd be toast."

She laughs. "True. Can you imagine a burly security guard pulling me to the side, TSA style, me emptying my bag and then a shiv tumbling out."

We both dissolve into a fit of laughter at that scenario playing out.

"So now you fully admit you've been carrying around a shiv?" I question teasingly.

"Fine, I will admit defeat on this one. You're right, Cohen." Her nose scrunches as if it physically pains her to admit I could be right.

"I should've recorded that. I could've edited it on a loop and made it my ringtone for you." Her nose scrunches further as she laughs.

"Do people even still mess with ringtones anymore?" she wonders aloud.

"You're right. They either don't call, or their phones are on silent," I concede.

We fall into amicable silence as we work on our task. The TV was already on when we walked in, but it's just ambient noise. As if snapping out of a trance, E glances my way.

"Hey, did you want to watch something?" she asks in a tone that suggests she's beating herself up for not being more hospitable even though I didn't come here to watch TV.

"Sure. What's your all-time favorite show?" I ask, preparing myself to not outwardly judge whatever answer she throws my way.

"Psych," she says without hesitation. E whips her head in my direction for confirmation. "Tell me you've seen it."

I hesitate, which only causes her eyes to widen. "I've only seen a few episodes here and there."

"Psych it is then," she wields the remote dramatically as if it were a presentation clicker and pulls up the show. "You're going to love it."

For the record, I was trying to pay attention, but not even Shawn flailing his arms around while making bird noises can distract me from stealing glances at her. She's relaxed, and laughter bubbles out even though I can tell she has seen this episode a thousand times.

I've got it down to a science—work, look, work, look. We're flying through and almost halfway done with the pile of mice when I decide to break the comfortable silence.

"Ok, you've converted me to a Psych fan. Do they have a fandom name?"

She smiles in my direction, trying not to laugh. "If you thought the names for our school events were cheesy..."

"Just tell me, now I have to know," I say as I try to read how bad this answer is about to be from her expression.

She's barely able to get it out with a straight face, but she tries to articulate, "Pysch-os." After a beat for it to register, we both can't hold it in any longer, and dissolve into laughter.

"That's so bad," I gasp.

"But so good," she finishes as we fall into a second round of revived hysterics.

Once the laughter slowly dies, we're left staring at each other, guards down, sitting closer than we were before. The Psych theme song is playing in the background, but I barely register it.

The shiv still hovers in her grip, and I slowly take it out of her grasp, our fingers brushing as I reach to set them down on the coffee table. This moment could turn into something very different if we still had those in our hands. I use the momentum of edging back on the couch to get closer until the sides of our thighs softly brush together.

She looks down at the contact, then back up at me with a look of shock and something I haven't seen before. We both slowly lean in, until we're teetering close enough for me to see the light dusting of freckles on her cheeks that I haven't seen up close. It is both jarring and exhilarating seeing a side of her that most people aren't privy to. I'm just about to close the gap, when we hear, "Honey I'm home," coming from down the hallway.

"I'm pretty sure you can only say that when you're actually walking in the door," I chide, not in the mood to deal with Jade as she strides our way.

"I'm pretty sure there aren't any rules that say differently. I was stuck in virtual after school tutoring, so I feel like I've just come back from school anyway." She looks between us, trying to hide her smirk. "Cohen, what're you doing here?"

Elle holds up a mouse, cord dangling, before responding. "Helping me."

Jade doesn't look convinced and just hums as she goes to the kitchen and starts clanging around. Moment ruined. We all chat about school, as the frustration with Jade's interruption wears off and we fall into easy conversation. Before I know it, we finish the task at hand, I eat dinner with them on the couch, and E is walking me to the door.

"Thanks for your help, Cohen," she says as she shuts the front door, leaving us alone and away from prying ears.

"Anytime. I had fun fixing mice, eating dinner with you guys, and becoming an official Psych-o."

She laughs. "Any luck on our catchphrase?"

I sigh. "The more I think about it, the emptier my brain gets." I feel like I'm letting her down with one of the few jobs that's solely mine in our investigative team.

Always somehow in tune with my thoughts, she encourages. "Don't worry, it'll come to you at the right time." I feel the instant rush of warmth at the brush of her fingertips on my arm as she squeezes in solidarity, smiling up at me. Using the momentum of her initiation, I pull my arm back, causing her to stumble forward a bit as I pull her into a hug.

Serotonin in the form of her naturally sweet scent hits me and it takes everything in me not to take a big inhale. My plan is to not pull back all the way, bend down, and finish what we started earlier.

Before I can bring it to fruition, she gently pulls away.

"See you tomorrow, Cohen," she says with a small wave.

"See you tomorrow," I reply, trying to hold in my grimace.

As I walk back to my unit, I scuff the ground with my toe in frustration. So much for making my move. My shoulders straighten in determination and I make a silent promise to myself to not let another chance pass me up.

CHAPTER TWENTY-ONE

Elle

After trying to recall every calming technique and coming up short with calming breaths, the 3-3-3 technique, and many others, I'm hoping that I can make the period go faster by sheer force of will. It's the day before Halloween, and all the students are in rare form today, but the freshmen are five seconds away from making me lose it.

I watch as one student looks around, head swiveling back and forth to check for onlookers, before slowly crumbling a candy wrapper that isn't supposed to enter my computer lab only to tuck it behind the desktop for me to clean up later. I walk over to the student, determined to maintain my composure.

"How's it going? Need any help?" I ask in standard greeting, voice an octave higher than usual.

"Nope, I'm just creating the next masterpiece. You'll have no choice, but to give this an A," he states as if this is an indisputable fact. Oh, to have the confidence of a teenager.

"As long as it follows the rubric, which I'm sure you've checked extensively," I respond, sarcasm lacing my words.

A flicker of panic crosses his face as he recovers. "Oooh yeah. I could probably recite it by now."

"I bet," I retort. "You were also going to throw that candy wrapper in the trash can and never bring food in the lab, right?" I say in a mock cheery tone.

He guffaws at me a second before grabbing the wrapper. "Yes, Ma'am."

I give him a genuine smile as I walk back. "That's why you're the best."

"You mean your favorite right?" he suggests.

"You know I don't have favorites," I retort as I pass by the other computers.

"Sure, you don't," another student mumbles. When she notices I've heard her aside, we both share a laugh. She shrugs and gets back to work. Just as I'm starting to calm down, another student slowly approaches my desk, SD card half stuck out of the slot in the DSLR camera.

This isn't my first rodeo, and I've learned that lecturing isn't an effective option, so I take more of the disappointed parent approach. Wordlessly, I maintain eye contact, mouth set in a straight line of disapproval, as I reach into my desk for the pliers I've learned to keep at the ready. I hold my hand out for the camera, pull out the SD card unscathed, and hand them both back to the student.

"What are we not going to do anymore?" I ask in a resigned, neutral tone.

"Get the SD card stuck in the camera," he replies guiltily.

"If the card isn't fitting, what should you do?" I ask to reinforce the point.

"Flip it," he answers.

"Exactly. Thanks for bringing it to me instead of trying to fix it yourself," I say, giving him a small mercy.

He seems to relax a bit as he weakly smiles and trudges towards the door to his group. All of whom have been staring wide eyed at our interaction making it clear that he drew the short straw or lost a game of nose goes, before bringing the problem to my attention.

As luck would have it, Ezra waltzes in at the moment, his knack for the worst timing annoying as always. I'm psyching myself up for an impromptu observation, until I notice the mug of candy he waves in my face.

"Hey, just wanted to stop by and wish you a Happy Halloween a day early from the CTE Department," he chimes.

I instinctively scoot back a bit and grab the mug. "Thanks, Ezra, I appreciate it," I add, plastering on a smile. He nods in approval and leaves the room.

A student snickers, "That dude is so weird."

Another chimes in, "I had him for English last year.""And?" They glance over.

"And I'm glad that's over," the surrounding students snicker.

"Be nice," I chide without heat. They shrug and get back to work.

It's like trying to push the laptop cart up a hill, as I try to gain momentum pushing Cohen towards Riley's room after school before we report for duty at the Halloween Carnival. He's digging his feet in and won't budge.

"Oh come on?! Why can't you be the one to tell him and I'll be right there," I reason.

He looks back, trying to shoot me a look, but we're still fighting each other as he holds his ground while I fail to move him another inch.

He lets out a humorless laugh. "E, it was your idea. I'm just there for moral support."

With that, he pushes forward to free himself of my grasp. Before I can process it, he's moving behind me to push me towards the door. I try to dig my feet in, but I can already feel myself sliding towards the door. Before we ruin the carpet, I relent and walk of my own volition. But not before I look back with a glare.

That earns me a smile, which is somehow even more annoying as I trudge towards his room. I don't want to know what it's like to be on the receiving end of a Riley lecture, but I have a feeling I'm about to find out.

"Hey, Riley. Can we talk for a second?" I ask as he looks up from the desk in his office.

"Sure, come in," he says matter of fact. I look back at Cohen. He nods in support and walks in with me.

I can feel myself start to sweat as I try to hype myself up for this conversation. Even though I'd rather not admit it, even to myself, knowing Cohen's right there makes me feel slightly better.

"We have something to conf—I mean —tell you," I start.

"You guys are dating, and you want me to know out of courtesy since my room is sandwiched between yours," he ventures.

My eyebrows pull together in confusion, "What? No."

"Oh," he says as an awkward silence descends upon us.

I steal a glance at Cohen, who's trying not to smile. Traitor.

"I'll stop guessing, what's up?" Riley tries again.

I clench my fists, steal a breath, and rip off the Band-Aid. "We have some information about the case."

I then proceed to fill him in on our conversation with an anonymous source, and to his credit, Riley listens, then takes a beat. "I don't know if you want to start a podcast, or have some kind of weird true crime fetish..."

"That's not it," I start.

"But—" Riley interrupts. "You need to get off the case. There is an actual person killing people, so I suggest you hold on to whatever self-preservation is buried deep in there and leave it to a professional." He gestures to himself.

Cohen takes this as his cue to finally join the conversation. "If any of the amateur sleuths on tv or podcasters that solved cold cases left it to the professionals, fewer cases would be solved." I can't tell if he's saying this with sarcasm, or as if this is somehow a valid point that will resonate with Riley, who laughs darkly. "And those TV sleuths would die a fictional death if the killer came after them or the podcasters, whose perpetrator is likely dead in a cold case. This killer is very much alive and there are real consequences."

He takes a deep breath and makes us stand in silence as it whistles out through his nose. "I'm willing to forgive the file cabinet incident, but I won't be as kind in the future. You two need to watch yourselves. You think you're being careful, but you're not. You have a target on your back with that Instagram account, and you never know what someone will document." He finishes his mini lecture and we exchange pleasantries and leave the room.

We gather our stuff, and Cohen insists on carrying it for me.

Once we're out of ear shot and on the way to our cars, Cohen starts, "Did he?"

"Not so subtly threaten us? Or warn us?" I glance over to see Cohen's wide eyes match my intensity.

"Yep," he finishes. Words are caught in his throat as he glances up to the ceiling in thought.

"You don't think... Riley's behind the Instagram account do you?"

A snort escapes me. "I don't think Riley even knows what a hashtag is. That man is a 30 something trapped in a 50-year-old's body. His entire file system is still paper. Plus, I doubt he has the time for that."

"True, it just seemed weird he brought it up."

Cohen nods in agreement as we keep trekking it out to the parking lot, not bothering to check out mailboxes as we breeze by the office.

We both go home to soak up the 2 hours we have left, deciding to ride to the event together. Even though I know it's the job of a teacher and is literally written in our contracts as, "all other duties as assigned," duty after a full workday makes it seem like an endless non-stop stretch. My brain is absolutely fried, but I've long become accustomed to pushing past exhaustion, to the point that I barely notice the way my eyes feel heavy, and the low hum of the heaviness settling in my body.

On the drive back to school, while I try to psych myself up, Cohen and I slip into easy conversation as we ask about each other's families. He makes me laugh with another story about his infamous family dinners. He's the youngest of four, a sister with a passion for romance novels, and two brothers always ready to mess with him.

As an only child, family dinners seem like something that would only happen in a movie, that I unabashedly see with rose colored glasses. We continue to chat for the rest of the car ride, and before we know it, we're already pulling up to the teacher lot.

We make our way to the front table to sign in and get our official instructions. This time we've been assigned to the same duty station. Haunted House monitors. "Haunted," is probably an exaggeration, but every year we block off the hallway to put up PVC pipe and fabric to close off the entire upstairs.

It transforms into one long stretch of Haunted House. The seniors are in charge of decoration and always try to outdo the class before them for ultimate bragging rights. One year, they even tallied how many freshmen were crying by the exit. This may seem like a barbaric tradition, but it is what it is and our job is to make sure no one actually dies.

I say as much to Cohen and he has the audacity to respond, bumping my shoulder.

"With your track record, that may be more of a challenge than you think."

Even though I know it's a joke, the rationale sends a knife through my heart, and I can't hide the look of shock and guilt that immediately transforms my features, erasing the smile that was on my face a moment ago. Seeing the physical impact of his words sends Cohen into an immediate backtrack. He sucks in a breath and clenches his pant legs at his sides.

"E, I'm sorry. I didn't mean it like that. I was just doing our normal back and forth and I didn't even think about what I was saying." Imploring me to understand his fumble.

"Yeah, you didn't think." I snip, unable to hide my true feelings. "But it's fine," I say, trying to gloss over this as we near our post at the end of the hall. I already feel like all the other teachers, sans Jade, think of me as a screw up, and now that Cohen is insinuating murder follows me everywhere I go, it's hard not to jump to conclusions.

Maybe we don't know each other as well as we thought. We just met at the beginning of the semester.

"It's not fine, and I want to talk this through," Cohen stands firm.

I sigh, a mix of defeat and frustration. "I don't want to cry while on duty, so can we do this later?"

"Fine. But we're talking about this on the way home," he declares.

Crap, I forgot he's my ride, so there will be no escaping this. Is this day over yet?

CHAPTER TWENTY-TWO

Cohen

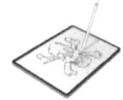

The look she tosses my way is a mix of hurt and frustration. We were just laughing and carrying on as usual until I put my foot in my mouth. Again. E power walks ahead of me to escape and talk to the other teachers volunteering, leaving me alone with my thoughts.

I try to calm myself. Obviously, it was just a bad joke. This one sentence won't tank our entire relationship. And if Elle was that fickle, and I know she's not, I wouldn't want to date her anyway. I mean, be friends/coworkers anyway. Whatever. I've said stupid stuff before, and I'll say stupid stuff again. Once she cools off, it'll be fine. But maybe I should wait to make my move? I'd like to think it's never been this hard before with anyone else, but maybe I've never cared this much before.

A spider drops down in front of my face, halting my internal monologue. I quickly swerve just out of its grasp, when I hear a maniacal laugh, and slowly glance up at a teacher tying the fishing wire from the ceiling. At least I'm not the only one who is delirious. It feels like opposite day with the seniors barking orders at their teachers, helping to execute their plan.

They're enjoying this power trip a bit too much. I slyly move closer to Elle. I'm two teachers away from her and Jade as they chat. Jade has to work the cake walk downstairs, but she's helping us in an attempt to spend more time with Elle. I can hear bits and pieces of their conversation from my vantage point.

"Miss, you're putting too much web in one spot. You have to spread it out better," a student instructs.

Jade gives the student a sharp look. "Mitchell, when you took my class, you never put this much effort into any of my projects. Why am I going to for yours?"

He smiles in spite of himself. "You're never going to let me live down that group project thing, are you?"

"Not in your lifetime." Jade smiles, saccharin sweet.

He walks away shaking his head slightly, laughing. "That's cold, Miss."

E and Jade dissolve into a fit of giggles as they continue their assembly line of Jade applying the web and E coming in behind with the fake spiders.

E cocks her head to the side, appraising their work. "I hate to say it, but..."

Jade shoots her a look. "I know, Mitchell was right, it does need some work."

I feel a pang of jealousy. The decorating process would fly by if I was able to chat with Jade and Elle. I fall into a tired lull, as I continue stringing lights, while listening to the easy back and forth between them. The easy back and forth that we used to have. I shake my head, mentally resetting myself. When I'm overtired, I tend to think of the worst-case scenario first. That's all this is. The staticky intercom jolts me back to reality as our shining beacon Pat McPatterson comes on over the loudspeaker.

"Come one, come all, to the annual Halloween Extravaganza. Check in at the front and explore the spooky haunts and grab a few treats while you're here. Every ticket purchased goes to the Scholars of Tomorrow fund, so help yourself to two caramel apples tonight. Have a spooktacular evening."

With that, he signs off in a cacophony of static, and the other teachers start removing the ladders and picking up the glue guns that litter the hallway, as we all make our way to our stations. In our tired stupor, we resemble zombies, shuffling through the school.

Once in my spot, I glance around at the product of our handiwork. A toe-curling sight, but as far as I can see, the walls are lined in a mixture of cheesecloth and fake web, with spiders embedded at every angle and a body shaped contraption is covered in fabric and fake web.

The seniors weren't too happy when the medical science teachers refused to let them use the expensive dummies as props, so they improvised. Black table clothes and construction paper on PVC pipe contain each section, and the overhead chicken wire arches at the top of one side to another are also completely covered in web, making it look as if the spiders are closing in at any second. A wireless speaker is hidden behind with the sound of leaky pipes and scurrying creatures to complete the overall ambience.

I know the other sections that extend beyond ours each have very specific themes. One has doll heads, and the theater students are dressed as creepy dolls sitting in these oversized chairs and stay completely still until someone comes near.

They tried it out on us, and I swear I saw a teacher almost have a heart attack as they screeched. Further back is a creepy hospital, a section that looks like their parents' lawn directions exploded, complete with a circle of illuminated witches, heads cast towards the ceiling, as if chanting the same imaginary spell.

They wouldn't let us see what's in the last section, and the seniors were very secretive about whatever it was. If we had our full wits about us, I'm sure someone would have demanded to see what it is, for fear it could be inappropriate, but technically their design was approved by the principal, so we just let it slide.

The overhead lights turn off and the faint sound of shrieks and laughter fill the halls as the kids are admitted into the event. E slides in next to me, so quiet I almost don't realize it. The smell of her fruity shampoo and the burst of serotonin that always hits my bloodstream the minute she's around, as if my mind knows before my eyes can catch up, are dead giveaways.

"Hey," I start.

"Hey," she responds, tone clipped. She's standing further away from me than normal.

"It turned out pretty creepy." I point out lamely, looking around.

"I wouldn't want to go through this thing," she concedes.

I glance her way. At least her face seems neutral. Small victories. "Not a haunted house person?"

"Definitely not. Are you?"

I shrug. "I mean I've done them with friends, but I don't seek them out."

She sucks in a deep breath through her nose, sighing as she turns to face me.

"Cohen."

"E?" I run a hand through my hair.

"I'm tired, you're tired. I know you didn't really mean what you said. Can we just forget this?" she says hopefully.

"For now, sure. But we're still talking in the car."

She groans.

"What changed your mind so quickly?" I was not expecting her to relent this easily.

"I know I wouldn't want you to hold me to something I said as a joke when I'm trying to get through duty, so I am extending you the same courtesy." She sends a small grin my way.

"Are you sure you don't want to skip the car conversation?" she says, giving me the most adorable sad eyes. If this weren't important to our relationship, then it would be working. My parents always told me not to let arguments fester, and I intend to apply their advice.

"You wish. No, you're not getting out of that," I chide, ruffling her hair. She bats my arm away playfully.

"Why not?" she asks with an innocent smile. Wow, she really is flipping through every evasive tactic in the book.

"Because, I know we need this. We had a conflict. That just means our goals didn't align. You seem to take conflict as a sign you've done something wrong. But, if we don't talk it out, that conflict will fester into miscommunication later."

"If the counselors are sick, I'll let them know you can fill in. That was astute." She bumps my shoulder, standing closer to me than when we first got to our stations. Relief floods my body as we return to our normal cadence. I didn't realize how much our tiff affected me.

"Thanks, that's years of therapy talking."

I can tell I'm about to get follow up questions after that flippant confession, but the first group of loud students makes their way towards us.

"Ms. Dannon!" I hear a voice screech as their eyes adjust, and they spot us.

"Hey, girls!" E says happily. I vaguely recognize them as the girls from the first day of school.

"Hi, Mr. Sinclair," one says. I'm shocked to be included in their little group, having never spoken to them.

"Hey," I respond.

They look between us and giggle. "You guys are working this together?"

"You get to hang out with your friends. Why shouldn't we?" E expertly deflects.

"Are you sure you're just friends?" her boyfriend says with a smirk, that sets the rest of the group into barely contained hysterics.

We both look at each other for a beat, then back to them.

"Yep, pretty sure," I say for both of us.

"Stop holding up the line," another student whines from behind them.

"Have fun, see you Monday," E addresses the group as she motions them forward.

"Bye, Miss D," they chant in unison.

E leans in to whisper in my ear, "They just had to try it, didn't they?!"

I whisper back, "They're teenagers, of course they did." We laugh and motion forward the next group of students.

"Favorite condiment?" I ask, head leaning against a locker, not caring that my hair is half tangled in the fake web.

E sways in her spot, trying not to fall asleep standing up. We have a sheen on our faces from the sweat and humidity of the stifling building and fog machine combination. The chalky smell with that undercurrent of syrupy sweetness stings our nostrils as the novelty of working the haunted house has long since worn off.

Our empty punch cups lay at our feet, and E donned the fake spider ring that garnished the top. She hasn't taken it off since. Jade was nice enough to bring us refreshments. She's the only one that remembers we're still here, as we both constantly check the bleeding red blinking clock that ticks painstakingly slow.

Thirty minutes to freedom. We're strung out from exhaustion, and have been inhaling this fog for hours. Yes, we already Googled the side effects of inhalation hours ago in a fit of boredom when there was a lull in patrons.

I glance over at E, expecting to see her slumped against the wall like me, but she's squinting into the distance, body rigid and alert.

"What's—" She shushes me, keeping her eyes trained on something. The haunted house entrance blocks my path, so I quietly slip behind her, a chill creeping slowly through my body. Bulky. Slumped. Still. A figure is sitting in one of the chairs, and he doesn't look conscious. His large shoulders are drooping to the left, causing his head to lull to one side following the slope of his body. Is finding a dead body synonymous with duty?

CHAPTER TWENTY-THREE

Elle

Nausea churns in the pit of my stomach as the sweet smell of the fog machine turns acrid, my focus shifting to the possible corpse facing away from us. A slight chill passes through my body, light as a breeze, and I zone in on the figure while the ringing in my ears slowly rises to a terrifying crescendo.

Cohen's arm brushes mine as we slowly inch forward, grounding me in the moment; a gentle reminder I'm not facing this alone. The blueish purple hue from the lights casts the scene in an eerie glow, and the fog brushes the bottom of the chair, moving past the shoes of the figure. We've nearly shuffled our way to the chair, and I'm dreading what we'll confirm when we get there. I can't think of another explanation other than a dead body.

I'm silently wishing that another person didn't meet their end at this cursed high school, when I have to push all thoughts aside to focus on the task at hand. Cohen and I lock eyes, and he nods twice, as we both lay a hand on either shoulder of the—I scream as the head topples sideways from the sudden force, breaking free from the top half to land on the floor with a thunk.

Wait. A hollow thunk.

With a breath I can't distinguish as frustration or laughter, Cohen murmurs, "Is that a freaking mannequin?" I dig through the layers of jacket and t-shirt to find a fabric center.

I huff out a dark laugh. "Yeah, it is." We both look at each other and smile with relief. A new wave of awareness washes over me as my senses are drawn to the electricity stemming from our joined hands. In all the commotion, we must've linked hands at some point. And this is not how you would guide a niece or nephew; this is the intertwined stuff of relationships. For some reason, I don't want to be the first to let go, but I'm not brave enough to squeeze in acknowledgement, so I opt for the chicken's way out and keep my appendages as still as possible.

Maybe he'll think I don't notice? He takes the lead, giving my hand a quick squeeze before letting go.

I've put this off. I've dreaded this moment. That's why I blinked and now I'm buckling my seatbelt, trying to mentally prepare my exhausted brain for this conversation with Cohen. I take my time fastening it, as if the few extra seconds I'm buying myself are precious. Cohen is adjusting my air vent towards me and doesn't notice. I suck in a breath as we pull out, and he gets on the road.

We're sitting in quiet, content silence, so I press my head against the cold window and try not to fall asleep; the flash of passing streetlights my only focus. After a few minutes, Cohen is the first one to break the silence.

"The first rule of having a conversation like this is that we're honest." He glances my way before continuing.

"Even if it isn't what we want to hear. Ok?"

"Ok." I agree with a nod.

"What are we doing?" he starts.

"Well, I'm just trying to get through the school year. I don't know about you," I confess.

He shakes his head, not willing to let this go. "No, I mean with us."

I decided to stop playing around and do something productive with this. It's only fair to both of us. Of course, I can still make him say something first. Before I'm vulnerable, I need some assurance he hasn't been flirting for fun and is just trying to clear the air because we work together.

I try not to choke on my spit, thinking about how embarrassing it would be if my feelings turn out to be unrequited. It would be so uncomfortable and he would probably ask for a new mentor.

"Well, what do you want from us?" I pry, putting extra emphasis on "us." I remove my cheek from the window, the ghost of the cold glass replaced with a lingering sting as I glance his way. I can only make out his general features as we get further into the mountains past any streetlights.

The moonlight and reflection of the headlights act as the only sources of light, casting his face in a partial glow. His expression is thoughtful, and his mouth is set in a straight line. I can't discern what feelings are swirling around in his mind before he speaks.

"Honestly, I like you E. Normally, I would have already asked you out by now, but I can't tell if you feel the same way. Sometimes I think you do, but maybe I've just been friend zoned." He keeps his eyes on the road but sneaks a glance at me every few seconds.

"Cohen. I like you too." It takes a beat for my words to hit him. Once they do, I can see his teeth glow in the light as he smiles. I have to remind myself to talk as I sit in shock, listening to the wind whipping the car in a steady rhythm. A pit settles in my stomach as I realize the reality of our situation. This would be very complicated for both of us.

"But," I start, watching his smile falter.

"We work together. Our classrooms are almost right next to each other. We live in the same unit in the same complex. And you're my mentee. While there aren't rules against it, it's not encouraged."

I take a deep breath through my nose before continuing. Cohen is leaning towards me slightly, as if not realizing he's angling my direction.

"If things go south, we would never get away from each other. We would have to face each other all day every day, and that terrifies me. I'm still trying to prove to admin that I deserve to be at the school, and I don't know what they'll think of this."

He sighs. "It sounds like you're making excuses."

I suck in a breath. "I'm just being realistic. I don't want to leave my school. Wilson is my school."

"This could be our school," he finishes, grabbing my hand and intertwining our fingers for the second time tonight. Only this time, it was on purpose. I squeeze his hand in response, smiling in spite of myself.

The rustle of my blanket and creak of the springs are the soundtrack of what's shaking up to be a sleepless night. No matter how hard I try to push it out of my thoughts, the events of the night are in a constant loop in my head. It's the film compilation I never asked for. After our heart to heart, Cohen walked me to my door and gave me a goodnight hug. I'm glad he didn't try to kiss me in that moment, because we were shrouded in a cloud of exhaustion, emotionally and physically.

The timing wasn't right. I mean, if he tried to kiss me I would have let him, but I understand our conversation in the car wasn't exactly romantic. His hand cupped the back of my head, and he kissed my temple, which may or may not have turned my insides into soup.

If I could stop replaying it and get some sleep, then I could face teaching tomorrow. Luckily, it's a Friday, but it's also Halloween and I can't go in tired. That's the last thing I remember before I finally fall asleep.

CHAPTER TWENTY-FOUR

Cohen

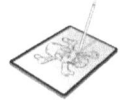

E lle adjusts the pearls on her Audrey Hepburn costume as she rattles off the names on her list, "Diana Fox, Mindy Arnold, Layla Jenkins, and Abby Holder."

The search for costumes that were comfortable enough to teach in was a struggle, but somehow we managed. Elle went with Audrey, and I decided to be a cactus. Basically, I bought a bright green sweatshirt and covered it in cut-up plastic straws to serve as the spines of the cactus.

I try to stifle a laugh, but the movement rattles the straws attached to my costume, scraping the desk. "Diana Fox? Really?"

Elle gives me a stern look that I would take seriously if a smile wasn't trying to break through the corners of her mouth, threatening to give her away.

"E, she's like 80 and she's been the school nurse for a million years."

She huffs defiantly. "Clearly, you haven't seen her when a student comes in and asks for a mint, just to get out of class. If looks could kill."

We both let out a laugh. We look ridiculous squished into our seats in our costumes, but we don't want to waste time changing. We're back at our place, AKA The Plot Thickens, for a planning session. The scent of coffee, mixed with the spicy hint of pumpkin, nutmeg, and cinnamon sets me at ease. A welcome break from the teenage body odor that's attacked my classroom and wins the battle against any air freshener I try.

It feels like we're in a hamster wheel of marking suspects off our person of interest list, unable to narrow anything down, but the suspect list is dwindling, so we should find a breakthrough soon.

She breaks my train of thought. "Ok, who's on your list?"

Glancing down, I recite from my screen, "Susie Tillman, Layla Jenkins, Brandi Daniels, and Tonya Brown."

Her eyes shine brighter as she says happily, as if we're not talking about murder suspects, "Hey, we both have Layla Jenkins on our list."

Layla Jenkins is the second year Math teacher, who is always trying to join our CTE inner circle. She's one of the few colleagues that's closer to our age and further away from retirement. She's also up Pat McPatterson's butt and spends all her time helping with Scholars of Tomorrow. She's the Resource and Records coordinator, meaning she takes care of the logistics once a scholarship is awarded to a student.

She also unofficially acts as the PTA treasurer and tallies up the cash at events. We always bring the cash from our stations to her at fundraising events. Also, the three times I've talked to her she's brought it up. In extensive detail.

"Why did you put her on your list?" E questions.

"She's at every function, she's one of the few on the PTA and Scholars of Tomorrow crossovers. I was able to get a hold of the attendance log from the minutes on their websites and cross referenced it to find the names."

Elle is digesting the information with a thoughtful hmmm. "I like that reasoning. Someone on the PTA and Scholars of Tomorrow committees would be familiar with the inner workings of the school, know both Mr. Anders and Pat, and attend everything."

"Does she seem capable of murder?" Elle asks, voicing her stream of reasoning.

We both look at each other for a minute and simultaneously say, "Yes."

I ask, "Why is she on your list?"

"Well, Layla is a teacher with access to all rooms and could easily plant the poison while we were all busy setting up, and I've heard rumors before that she's inflated student scores, and all sorts of stuff." She sighs. "It's just an overall feeling. Ya know?"

I nod. "Yeah. It's not any isolated thing, but altogether it looks sketchy."

"Exactly!" she says with a smile. We both stare at each other with matching smiles for a beat too long.

"Wait, why don't you ask her on a date?" she suggests.

My eyes widen in terror, and I choke on my spit. Mid coughing fit, I manage to choke out. "I'm sorry?"

"A date would be an easy way to get information out of her without spooking her."

"I didn't date any of the other suspects. Why her?" I ask defensively. My costume is starting to get oppressively hot. I tug at my collar, trying to get any air flow.

Her eyes are shining, and her earnest expression twists my heart. "Cohen, I have a feeling about her. I don't want her to shut down like Mr. Joesph."

I sigh and run a hand through my hair. If I thought there was another option that would work, I'd be all over it. My mind is coming up blank. "Fine. I'll do it." Her instant grin and little dance she does in her seat steels my resolve to go through with this ridiculous plan.

Looking over my shoulder, her smile is wiped clean in an instant, and her shoulders bob up as she straightens.

Nodding in that direction she says, "No time like the present."

I slowly turn around to see Layla Jenkins trying to decide what to order from the menu. I should buy a lottery ticket, because what are the odds?

I steal one last glance at E to give her a chance to back out, but she nods towards Layla's direction, and I realize I have no other choice. Guess I'm actually doing this.

I slowly walk over, trying to seem like I'm not making a beeline for her. Layla is tall and one of the few people I don't have to look down at. Her brown curls take up most of her face and her pale skin almost glows. She's cute, but she can't hold a candle to Elle. That's like comparing an off-brand pencil to a Ticonderoga. I walk up behind her and decide to come off casual.

"Hey."

Layla whips around, a big smile dominating her features once she registers my presence. "Oh hey, Cohen. What're you..." Her smile falters as she registers Elle at our table. "You're on a date with Elle." She starts to turn back around to the menu.

"Nope. We're not on a date. We're just friends," I say, hoping the week I spent in theatre in high school is paying off.

She glances back at me, eyes narrowed. "Really?"

I put my hands in my pockets, so I can't fidget in my lie. "Yep, we're just in the middle of a mentor/mentee planning session. That's it."

Not fully convinced, Layla questions, "Huh, I heard from like everyone that you're a couple."

I let out a small laugh. "You know how the rumor mill is. Once they get a hold of something, they won't let it go."

This seems to placate her, and her features instantly soften. "That's true. So why did you come over here?"

"I was wondering if you wanted to grab dinner sometime?"

"A date? With you?" Layla questions, voice a mix of skepticism and an octave higher than normal.

"Yep," I answer, not sure if I'm about to get turned down.

"Sure," she answers without hesitation once she realizes I'm serious.

"Really?" I clarify, incredulous.

"Oh yeah. You're super hot," she states as if it's an indisputable fact.

"Uh, thanks." That's not the answer I was expecting, and I thought this would take more convincing.

Without hesitation, she grabs a coffee sleeve and pulls a sharpie out of her teacher bag. "Here's my number. Text me the details."

"Ok, see you later," I say with a wave.

She smiles and steps into the coffee line. I walk back to E and our table. She is trying to act as if she wasn't watching our entire conversation and looks too engrossed on whatever is on her laptop. As soon as I plop back down, her eyes shoot up to meet mine.

"Sooo, I saw smiles, is that a yes??"

"Were you watching our entire conversation?" I ask with a raised brow.

"Of course," Elle says unabashedly.

"It's a date." I answer with a lack of enthusiasm.

"Yay, that's great!" she says and we high five. I glance back towards the line and notice Layla watching our exchange with a soft smile. I'm the only one not smiling. This wasn't the big move I was planning. Taking another girl out on a date. I sit back down at our command station that's scattered with papers, drinks, and teacher bags resting on the floor.

"E, I'm going on a date." I blanch. "With a murderer."

She pats me on the shoulder, the excitement from moments ago fading faster than a Chromebook battery. "Murder suspect," she clarifies.

CHAPTER TWENTY-FIVE

Elle

I don't like this. I don't like this. I don't like this. I tighten my ponytail with a tug, trying to distract myself from the fact it's D-Day. Yep, tonight Cohen and Layla will be on their date. I can't help but feel she stole my date, but I have no one to blame but myself.

I pushed him into this. And as much as I keep telling myself I want to be friends, clearly after our conversation at the Halloween carnival, that wasn't the direction we were heading. Until I stalled us out. It might be good for the case, but it's not good for me.

I try to focus on anything else as I make last-minute adjustments to my slides and fold copies for today's activity. My noise-canceling headphones are buried deep in my desk drawer.

I don't have the luxury of using them during the day, but I keep them stashed away like the supersize bag of M&Ms in Jade's desk drawer. As soon as I hear the opening cadence of my favorite true crime podcast, I can feel my shoulders ease and lean into the episode.

Cohen and I unbuckle our seatbelts as we arrive at the restaurant for his date. We pull out our phones and he calls me. The feedback screeches through the stale air of the car, causing us both to wince before muting the call.

Cohen is still rubbing his ear when he checks. "Ok, I'll have the phone in my jacket pocket, so you can hear us." "You're recording this, right?"

"I am now," I confirm. Cohen lets out a humorless laugh. "If we get caught—"

I settle further into my seat. "We won't get caught. Don't say that."

He slides his phone into his pocket and straightens his jacket. "Wish me luck," he says with a nervous smile.

"Good luck," I say with false brightness, mumbling to myself as he gets out. "Not too much luck."

"Huh?" he asks, sticking his head back in for a second, one hand on the car door, and the other resting on the frame.

"I said good luck," I clarify, reaching for my stake out snacks, while trying to balance my phone.

He walks around the car, opens my door, and leans in, meeting my eyes. "No, you said something after that," he states, brow furrowed.

"Weird, I don't remember what it was," I lie with a shrug, still struggling to open my snack package. He snatches it from me, opening it with ease, and hands it back to me. I mumble a thanks, as I try not to look him in the eye.

He pats my leg to get my attention, and my whole body stiffens, on high alert. I slowly meet his gaze, noticing we're close enough to breathe the same air. I can smell the mint from his gum and I wring my hands in my lap, trying, but failing to play it cool.

"You know I'm only doing this because I have to," he implores.

"Yeah, I know." I hum in agreement.

"If I had a choice, I wouldn't be taking Layla on this date," he confesses.

"Oh?" I ask, trying to hide my smile.

He grins in return, not holding back. I sigh internally, cursing the boyish charm radiating from his unbridled flirtiness. We're so close, and it takes everything in me not to close the distance, but he can't show up to his date with Layla wearing my lipstick. Before either of us has a chance to act, fate intervenes as his alarm pierces the air around us, causing us to jump.

Luckily for me, I catch my snack bag before it spills all over his front seat, while he yelps in pain as he bangs his head on the car. Our moment ruined, I see the disappointment in his eyes as he resigns himself to the task at hand while fumbling to turn off the piercing alarm.

"I'm going in. Don't want to be late," he says as he waves with his phone in hand, shutting the door and locking the car as if I'm not there.

After a few calming breaths to bring my heart rate back to normal, I recline the seat all the way back, balancing the phone on the middle console, trying to relax. Only to drop my phone under my seat.

Once I do some acrobatics to retrieve it, I clumsily grab the phone and set it back in its place with the only hand not covered in chip dust. The five seconds that have passed feel like hours, so I can already tell, this is going to be awhile.

CHAPTER TWENTY-SIX

Cohen

My palms are sweating. Why are my palms sweating? Oh, that's right. It's because E made me go on a date with a murderer. I'm silently contemplating how I got into this mess when I spot Layla, sitting in the entrance, fixing the hem of her dress, crossing and un-crossing her legs.

Dread sinks in my stomach as the enormity of the situation hits me as hard as a tin water bottle falling on the classroom floor.

This isn't a game for Layla. She thinks it's a real date. She's nervous. What kind of jerk does this to another person? Me apparently. I make a mental note to never cross my principles in the name of crime solving again, as I make my way towards her.

"Hey, Layla," I say casually, making sure to identify anyone I ad-dress for E's sake.

Her head whips in my direction and she smiles, shoulders dropping with the breath she exhales. Is she relieved? Did she think I was going to stand her up? We literally work together. That would be so awkward to ask someone on a date, ditch them, and then stand next to them during lunch duty for the rest of your career.

"Hey, you look great," she says, glancing up at me.

"Oh, uh you too," I stammer. I underestimated the difficulty of not sounding too interested since E was listening in, but also not making her think I was an idiot who can't talk to a girl. It's a mind game having the girl of your dreams listening in on a date with someone else. After we're seated, the realization that I'll have to keep the conversation up for the entire date hits me and I want to throw up.

It doesn't help that I'm picturing a certain blonde sitting across from me instead. Trying to put her at ease, I decide to get her talking about herself.

"So, Layla. What are you passionate about?" She taps her menu with her blood red claws before meeting my eyes.

"Ooh, well, when I'm not teaching or doing Scholars of Tomorrow stuff, I make miniatures," she starts excitedly.

My brows scrunch in confusion, "I'm not familiar. Miniature what?"

She laughs. "Anything really. Miniature bookshelves with tiny books, or kitchens with tiny food. It's just a good way to turn your brain off."

Unsure where to direct the conversation from here, I say the first thing that comes to mind. "Have you made a miniature of your classroom?" I ask with a smile.

Her cheeks flush as she looks down at the tablecloth, "Yeah, I already have."

"Do you have a picture?" I inquire.

Her face lights up as she digs in her purse for her phone. "Really?" she says almost breathless.

"Sure," I finish, glancing around the restaurant in search of an answer. Why is she acting like I just offered her a lifetime supply of flair pens?

Knifelike red nails block the corners of the screen as a grainy image of a classroom, her tiny classroom, comes into view as I squint to see in the shadows of the candlelight. Tiny, felt desks are lined up perfectly, and there's even a tiny plant sitting on the desk at the front. I sit up in my seat, mildly impressed. "Woah, that looks like your room."

You would think I crowned her teacher of the year, by the smile she gave me. I decide to pounce on her goodwill and get to the root of my task.

"I don't know how you have time to do stuff like that with all the hours you put in at Scholars of Tomorrow. What do you do with that again?"

"Oh, I'm the Resource and Records Coordinator. Meaning, when we have a fundraiser or we award the scholarship, I handle the logistics and money to make sure the correct amount is sent to the recipient and keep records of everything."

"So the money goes right to you? I'd be nervous handling that much cash all the time." Trying not to make my information digging obvious.

"Kind of. It goes through Pat, then me. He's so sweet and handles the cash box at all events, so I don't have to be at every single one. Then, I just have to keep track of everything until I take it to the school treasurer to put in our scholarship account."

She shakes her head and redirects her gaze towards me.

"I've been talking about myself way too much. Tell me more about you. What do you do when you're not at school?"

I open my mouth to answer, when a muffled noise. To my horror I realize it's E singing an off-key version of the chorus to *I Don't Care* by Charlie XCX.

In the haste to make the noise stop, I whip out my phone and end the call. Not before Layla has a full view of my screen and the caller ID.

"What the—" A glass shatters from a stunned waiter, drowning out Layla's choice words.

"Why is she listening to our date?" Layla shrieks. Her eyes go dark and she glares at me, "Is this some kind of dare or something?" "No it isn't like that I promise. It's—" Before I can finish my sentence, she cuts me off.

"Whatever, I don't wanna hear it." She spits, sarcasm dripping from her voice as she snatches her purse and leaves the restaurant. "You two deserve each other."

Well, lunch duty just got really awkward.

CHAPTER TWENTY-SEVEN

Elle

O nce Layla peels out of the parking lot, I exit the car with shaky hands, entering the restaurant in a haze of disbelief, still trying to reconcile the fact that my plan backfired so spectacularly. Mentally preparing myself for a lecture from Cohen, I make my way over to the table, but he just looks defeated.

His eyes are fixed on the tablecloth, instead of the gawking patrons, who are trying not to stare, but glancing his way every few minutes. Why did this plan seem like a good idea?

"Hey," I start, weakly sliding into Layla's empty seat. Evidence of her meltdown is evident in the askew tablecloth, that I right with a few tugs. Cohen's arms are resting on the tablecloth, and the subtle jolt alerts him to my presence. He glances up at me with a sad smile.

"I'm so sorr—" He cuts me off.

"Don't. We both agreed to do this." He sighs, straightening in his chair to face me. The reality of our situation becomes crystal clear, because from this vantage point — a fancy candlelit dinner with Cohen on the other side of the table, eyes glinting as the light catches the depth of his irises — this is what a date with him would look like. And I inserted myself into it. *Idiot.*

"We might as well eat. Our drinks aren't even here yet. Perfect timing," he suggests. I can tell he's trying to rally, settling into a new demeanor that my hopeful brain doesn't want to recognize.

"Perfect timing because I ran your date out. But sure, we'll go with that." I place her napkin on my lap and try not look giddy as I play with my hands under the table. "Before we forget this ever happened, I want to explain. I dropped my phone and I bet I wasn't paying attention and took it off mute. I was just listening until that song came on and I had to join in. I never meant for this to happen."

Cohen confesses, "I know you well enough to understand it was an accident. You know she wasn't really my date. Or not the person I wanted to be here." I hum in acknowledgement, trying to read his body language. It's open and he's facing toward me, making eye contact as he says it.

There's nothing to indicate deception. I think. Maybe I need to do more research before I can come to anything conclusive, though. Trying to pull us away from anything serious, I change the subject. "What drink did she order?"

He responds flatly, "Pepsi."

I grimace, while he huffs out a laugh. "Ew. It would never work out between you two on soda preferences alone. You're laughing, because you're not the one that has to drink it."

"True. I made the better choice," he concedes. The glint in his eyes indicates a double meaning to that statement. At that the fizzy, dark colored perfection, otherwise known as Dr. Pepper, is slid in front of Cohen, while I'm stuck with its off-brand cousin, Pepsi.

In an act of pure heroism, without a second thought as soon as the waiter walks off, Cohen swaps our drinks before I can take a sip. I start to protest, but Cohen jumps in. "Let me take one for the team."

"I think you already took one for the team," I point out.

"What's one more?" He shrugs, a soft smile on his face as he takes another sip. I can see the moment the liquid hits his tongue, as the smile transforms into a grimace. He pushes the cup away, as if reminding himself to tread lightly, before turning his attention back to me.

On most of my previous dates, this is where the conversation gets awkward. After the initial excitement and random small talk is when I crash and burn. There's one thing I underestimated about this date, though. *Cohen.* I'm trying to mentally recall every game of twenty questions I've ever played, as my mind is frustratingly blank. It's as if my brain were an Etch a Sketch that someone shook out in a huff.

Cohen takes over—thank God—and saves me from my thoughts.

"What are your plans this weekend?" he inquires as if I actually do interesting things on the weekends.

"Oh." I try to buy myself time before responding truthfully. "Well. I'll probably catch up on some grading." *I will finish all my grading.* "Then, Jade and I will make our annual pilgrimage to the pumpkin patch." *If I'm not a braindead zombie from grading and push it to next weekend. Like I've done the past two...* "What about you?"

"Honestly, I feel like I'm drowning, so I'll probably use this weekend to catch up. I do want to do all that fall stuff too, but there's not enough time." He rewards me with a self-deprecating smile.

"At least we're both spending our weekend the same way," I offer.

I'm about to jump in with offers of help as his mentor, but he continues before I have a chance. "You know who must be winning at this whole teaching thing?"

I lean forward in my seat, curious to see where this is going. "Who?"

He tries to stifle a smile. "Herald. I mean, who has time to create their own superhero?"

Choking on my spit, I try to answer through the cough, laughing. "I don't think Environmental Science Man will be a Marvel movie anytime soon. But the way he must've hand sewed the plants on that cape was wild." When he waltzed in wearing a homemade, custom costume, the rest of us put some distance between us to avoid comparison.

Wearing a black dress and pearls and calling it Audrey Hepburn was a bit on the lazy side, but it works. Cohen's cactus was at least more creative.

"I was trying to decide what would be comfortable to teach in," Cohen huffs out, clearly impressed with his dedication to the perfect costume, "but he wasn't. At all."

"I still think you should've leaned into the Flynn Rider thing."

"Whatever. You wish." I don't bother to tell him I actually do wish he would have worn that costume, but there's always next year.

We fall into the most comfortable back and forth, and I find myself forgetting this is technically our first date. We're both talking so much, it's hard to eat our food while getting sucked into conversation.

As we make our way to the car, a soft dread fills me that this is over. That dread is pacified as we're walking close enough that our arms and hands keep brushing. I can't decide if I'm purposefully veering in his lane to continue our streak, or if he's contributing, too. Something tells me both. We near the car, but neither of us makes a move to get in. The hum of the streetlights and chirps of the crickets act as our soundtrack as we face each other.

The cool autumn breeze is the only reason chill bumps cover my arms. As we stand in each other's space, I consider doing something—anything—when Cohen makes the first move. He puts his hands on my arms, bringing us impossibly closer.

I can feel the warmth of his breath on my nose as he speaks softly, "I have an idea for our catchphrase."

The haze slowly overtaking my senses comes to a crashing halt as I remember the task I gave him months ago. "What?" I ask with an incredulous huff.

Undeterred by my confusion, he continues, "It's so cheesy it just might work."

"It's kind of ironic how annoyed you get with Wilson's cheesy event names, but yet, you say the lamest things sometimes," I point out.

He shrugs. "Well, I'm only cheesy with you."

"What do you mean?" I wonder.

"Do you see me joking around with Riley? Or Jade? Or Herald?"

I stammer, "Well no. But—"

"Exactly," he says before continuing. The feel of his thumbs circling my arms breaks through his words, setting my brain at ease.

Leaning into the ridiculousness of the moment, I chide, "Let's hear it then."

On a dramatic inhale, he waits a beat before starting. I can see the slight blush on his cheeks as he continues. "Partners in crime." His smile breaks through and his inflection hints at an unfinished sentence. "All of the time," he finishes.

My gaze turns thoughtful as I try on the phrase, "Partners in crime, all of the time."

While I'm distracted, Cohen covertly moves his hand to cup my cheek and I register a small, triumphant smile, before he presses his lips to mine. The kiss is sweet and slow, and I feel it all the way to my toes. This moment feels momentous, and you can't convince me an applause track shouldn't be playing like an old sitcom. Maybe this moment is better suited for a rom-com.

We both break away for a second to appraise each other. Our faces are still close, but a safe distance away, so we haven't broken our hold. I can't quantify what we're looking for, but we both find it, as we lean in to continue, him catching my bottom lip, creating a sharper contrast to the gentle kiss moments before. If you're sitting there wondering if we're making out in a parking lot, it's not what I would have envisioned either, but it will now and forever be my favorite lot. Sometimes the most random spots or mundane things can transform with the right person.

He continues to intensify the kiss, and I continue to let him, our push and pull turning into a rhythm. On the road just beyond the parking lot, a car lays on their horn, jolting us out of our moment in a manner akin to a jump scare in a horror movie. Cohen keeps his hold on me, sliding down my arms to grip my hands as he looks around for the source of the commotion.

After realizing it wasn't in our vicinity, he wordlessly squeezes my hand and closes our distance to the car, opening my door for me to get in. I slide into the car, and he gets in the other side. He starts the car and takes off, beginning our trek home. He does this all—you guessed it— wordlessly. As in, no words come out of his mouth. The radio feels deafening and the only reason I don't completely lose it is because he reaches for my hand and intertwines our fingers.

Every so often, his thumb will brush my knuckles. The silence gives space for my thoughts to roam free. Which is never a good idea. Is this hand holding a consolation prize? Like, that kiss was terrible, and I don't want to be with you, and we should stay co-workers only, but I can at least hold your hand?

I know I could be the one to break the silence, but at this point, I feel like it's somehow a sign of defeat to speak first. So I don't. Like the mature adult I am.

As we reach the door of my apartment, I finally crack. "Ok, out with it."

Cohen stops and turns to face me, brows crinkling. "Out with what?"

"What was it? What about our kiss turned you off?" I take a deep inhale before continuing. "Is this your way of telling me we should just forget the parking lot?"

"Woah." He shoots me a perplexed look. "What gave you that idea?"

"You haven't said anything. Not. A. Word," I punctuate.

He looks stricken as the realization hits him. "I'm an idiot."

I level him with a look. "I'm not going to disagree." A slight smirk peeks through despite my better judgement.

He closes the distance and wraps me in a hug. Am I the idiot? My brain rationalizes this as yet another mixed signal. My voice comes out a muffled huff as I speak into his chest. "You never answered the question." This was worse than trying to make copies before your next class, only to realize the last person left the copier jammed.

He pulls back slightly, one hand on my shoulder, the other cupping my cheek.

"I wasn't second guessing anything. I was thinking about how much I like you." He gives my shoulder a squeeze and steps closer, closing the distance. Before I can get my bearings, Cohen brushes his lips to mine.

"Night, E," he calls as he strides towards his apartment with a wave.

"Night," I respond in a daze, still standing in front of my door.

How am I supposed to go through a normal school day after that?

Chapter Twenty-Eight

Cohen

I could pass for a circus performer as I try to carefully juggle two boxes of donuts and a catering box of Chick-fil-a. I'm almost home free as I grab my keys from my lanyard in front of my door and sift through the extra keys on my keyring until my fingers graze the six-prong beauty that will finally allow me to free my arms that are starting to cramp from holding them at such an awkward angle.

My vision is covered in grease-stained boxes, so when a hand pops up over the boxes and shoots down just as fast as if the owner jumped up and down, I nearly crawl out of my skin.

What's worse is when I stop and peer around the food tower a giant, knowing smile awaits me. "I thought you said you didn't do bribes?" Elle chides.

I appreciate that she knew I would be nervous on observation day, and when she messes with me, it does take my mind off it. Observations are where outside veterans watch a portion or whole class to see how you teach, interact with students, manage class behaviors, and offer tips in the form of a report card that lives in your file. Since I didn't go to college for education, I had to get alternative certification, meaning an outsider came in to observe an entire class period, and decide whether I was worthy of a teaching certificate before I could be official.

It was easy to say I would never bribe my students. In fact, I was actively appalled at her for even suggesting it when I asked for observation tips. But then it hit me like a spitball to the face, these students control my future. If the observer from Bright Futures, my teaching program, doesn't like what he sees and gives me a failing score on my observation, all the tests I took, hours of online modules that make you want to stick your hand in an old school pencil sharpener, and observation hours are for nothing.

My teaching license for alternative certification can be voided if I can't prove my skills to a random person with a clipboard who yields all the power. Suddenly, a bribe sounded like insurance that my career wouldn't go up in flames. That's how I ended up here. Buying my students' behavior with food. I offered donuts, and they raised me Chick-fil-a. Apparently, they keep a list of new teachers, so they know how far to push the limits. Even though I'm surprised they can put this much effort into a list of new teachers, but not turn in assignments on time, I'm slowly starting to learn that high school students—correction— probably all students can be relentless when they deem a task worth their time.

Of course, I can't admit defeat and have to keep some level of decorum, so I say. "What? This isn't a bribe, it's just motivation for them to be the best they can be. It's actually a reward."

Her mouth twitches and I can tell she is debating whether to call me on it. Instead, she just shrugs and says, "A reward, got it," and takes the boxes from my hands, so I can open the door.

Things have been different for us since the kiss. Or at least for me they have. We hadn't really talked since last night, and this purgatory of not knowing where we stand is killing me. As Elle walks past the door, I hold it open for her, catching a whiff of the shampoo with a peachy undertone that haunts my dreams. This doesn't seem like the time for answers, I think, sighing internally. She immediately gets to work, arranging the boxes for ease of serving. Her back is to me, giving me the perfect vantage point. She doesn't see me coming as I silently come up behind her, lightly tugging the belt loop of her slacks to pull her backward with me.

She startles in surprise, not ready for the interruption, as she wordlessly moves with me. My classroom couldn't have more windows if it tried, a typical awkwardly narrow space with doors at either end outfitted with, you guessed it—windows. There is a spot right in the middle that is out of view, which I used to my advantage. In hindsight, it was an incredibly stupid thing to do when anyone could walk in, but at that moment, I couldn't think about anything else. As I pull her closer, I notice a flash of shock register before I close the distance.

Even though our kiss is relatively quick, the world melts away. Noise dulls like a steady flow of music only coming through one headphone, and everything is hyper focused on her. She pulls away first. A look of shock clouding her features as she registers her surroundings. She shakes herself out of it and walks toward the door.

Luckily for us, she was on her way in when I stopped her, so she grabbed a makeup wipe from her purse, sliding back into our hidden spot to wipe off any evidence of lipstick while I'm not as quick and still struggling to get my bearings after we pull apart. Her breathing is quicker than usual, signaling she was as affected as I was. She is just better at hiding it. The pressure from her thumb on my jaw as she angles my face to check her work grounded me in our moment.

"We can't do this here ever again," she warns, looking me dead in the eye, jaw set.

My heart deflates as I process her words, and I can feel the crease settling in my brow, "Uh ok," is all I can mumble shakily.

Her eyes soften. "I don't want us to get fired, and PDA at school is a fast track to that."

I turn my back to her as I walk toward the food, so that I could pretend to finish setting up. "Yeah, sure. Got it."

I don't mean to be short with her, but I can't help the knee jerk reaction that springs forth to combat the sting of rejection.

"Cohen," she pleads.

"E," I manage in an even, bored tone.

"I don't want it to be this way. But it has to be." She chokes, and even though I can't see her face, I know she's trying not to cry. That sound cuts through my need to save face and I lower the façade. Just a bit.

I prod. "Are we still on for The Plot Thickens after school?"

I can hear the smile that breaks through. "For research on the case of course."

"Of course," I confirm, smiling in spite of myself.

"And an excuse to spend more time with you," She says in a tone close to a whisper.

"Really?" I perk up like an overeager puppy.

"Yeah." She grins, eyes bright.

"Partners in crime?"

"All the time."

Maybe, just maybe, cheesy phrases were growing on me.

The routine of settling down in our spot at The Plot Thickens, surrounded by the smell of coffee and books is quickly becoming my new
favorite thing. It doesn't hurt that one of my favorite people was across
from me too.

"How was your observation?"

"Fine."

"Seriously, that's all I get? How was it really?" Her brow crinkles
as she takes a gulp of air before continuing, "Did someone throw
something? Cuss you out? Did every student pull out their phones
and ignore you?"

I start. "Well, I mean the phone thing happens to everyone." She
nods in agreement. "But nope. It was fine. No one did anything other
than answer my questions."

"So that sounds better than fine."

"Well." I inhale before continuing, and E leans closer, as if she'll be
able to hear my words a second earlier if she closes the distance. "The
observer wouldn't stop tapping his pencil."

"Tapping his pencil?"

"Yeah. And he never smiled. Not once." I shoot a worried look her
way, as I see patience and understanding mirrored back at me. I have
her undivided attention. She isn't slyly typing out emails or adding to
lesson plans like usual. She's just waiting for me to continue.

"It's like I was doing something wrong. But I can't figure out what
it was."

She considers this for a moment. "Now that I think about it, my
observer never smiled either. I still got a good score, but she looked as

if she was getting a root canal the entire time. Maybe it's just part of their job description?"

I laugh. "Maybe."

With that, we get to work in companionable silence. After a bit, she starts as if she has to convince herself to break the silence. "So I've been thinking."

"Ok," I respond, turning my attention to her.

"You're not going to make a joke about that?" She prods.

Shaking my head, I explain, "No, you're the smartest person I know, so why would I?"

"Wow, now you're just trying to get on my good side." She smirks.

With a look of mock hurt, I turn my puppy dog eyes on her, "I thought I was already on your good side."

"To be determined," she chides playfully. I take advantage of our legs almost brushing by putting my hand on her knee under the table. Her face breaks into a bright smile and we both laugh. Even though we already had the conversation that in-school PDA was off the table, it's nice to have further confirmation that outside of school PDA is encouraged.

I see the transition on her face, as she switches to business mode. "So, we've made progress in the investigation."

"Have we?" I wonder.

Her face falters for a second, as if she's not convinced. "Well, we've ruled out suspect after suspect."

"But are we closer to a resolution?" I'm not trying to be difficult, just realistic. I'm not sure where she's going with this.

E shrugs. "I don't know. But I think we need to try a different angle."

"Like?" I lean forward, curious to know what she has in mind.

"Well, we haven't done much research on Mr. Anders himself. We've ruled out suspects, but have we focused on why someone would want to hurt him specifically?"

"That feels like something we should've started with," I reason.

"Yeah, we're amateurs. Now we'll know for the next time."

I jolt in reaction to her statement. "Next time?"

She ignores me and continues. "That's why I'll start digging into Mr. Anders, and I need you to research the poison in his mac and cheese. Maybe that will give us something we can use."

It feels like we're just hoping there is an invisible string we can pull that would lead us closer to the killer. But it's worth a shot. Over the next hour, I feel like I could have a minor in poisons and know more than I ever thought possible.

Just one more reminder of how terrifying the internet can be. The killer had all this information handed to them on a silver platter. Anyone could DIY this stuff.

"I'm learning so much about poison, but I will be clearing my search history after this." She laughs and listens while scrolling through her own findings. I continue, "We know from the autopsy report that the poison used was Ethylene Glycol, which is the main ingredient in antifreeze." I say sighing. "Which unfortunately is a common item, and tells us nothing about the killer."

"But..." I trail off dramatically. "While it's a fast-acting poison, it takes anywhere from 1-4 hours for symptoms to kick in, and even longer to kill you.""So it doesn't make sense that he reacted immediately..." Elle ponders aloud.

"Unless he was poisoned earlier in the day," I supply.

"But they tested the mac and cheese and it had traces of Ethylene Glycol, at least according to the report."

"Yeah, but maybe that was the dose meant to finish him off. Meaning, even if you noticed it at the Back 2 Cool event, we were still too late. There was no saving him."

"I guess," Elle concedes, still not sold on the idea.

Driving the point home, I continue. "E, you can't save everyone. You weren't the one to poison him, and it looks like he wasn't poisoned the first time in your presence. That last dose in the mac & cheese was probably overkill. You understand that, right?"

With a sigh she drags her eyes up to meet mine. "Yes, I understand. I would rather feel guilty for not noticing the poison versus feeling helpless."

"But that's why we're solving this. You were never helpless," I point out.

Instead of responding, she just smiles, a faint glimmer of hope flickering in her eyes. We return to our computers for a few quiet minutes. I sneak a few glances her way, but she's deep in thought.

"Speaking of the Back 2 Cool event," Elle mummers. "The minutes say they only raised $1,500 that night, but that doesn't seem right."

"Wait, you're right," I trail off. "The auction was right next to the committee sign up sheets, and that had to have raised at least $1,000 minimum."

E jumps in, "Then, the Scholars of Tomorrow donation box was full, which had to have been close to $400."

I finish, "And the concession stand sold out of sodas. Riley was working it and complained how he had to deal with a bunch of angry parents the next day."

Elle's fingers fly over her keyboard. "The football boosters run the concession stand and I bet I can find their minutes." After a few minutes of intense silence, she confirms, "Holy crap. They made $500."

I conclude, "So at the absolute minimum that's $1,900, which is at least $400 short from the reported amount."

"Wait, let's check another event to see if there's a pattern," Elle says. We shift through the minutes only to find concrete evidence that amounts ranging from $100 - $400 weren't matching up for months.

"Which means, someone's skimming off the top?" Elle says in shock.

I start, "Ok, so money is collected, and stays in the cashbox."

Elle chimes in, "Then, it's stored in the cashbox until the end of the night, where the tally is recorded on paper. Afterwards, the treasurer takes it to the school secretary to lock up and transfer it to the school account."

I wonder aloud, "Who's the treasurer that has the cash box and signs off on the final tally before the cash box goes to the school secretary?"

Elle contemplates it for a minute. "Well, Margot's on maternity leave, so Layla is the interim treasurer." We both look at each other with wide eyes. "Well, that's weird," she says.

Putting it to rest for now, I nod towards her laptop. "Any luck with the Anders research." She huffs. "Not really." "We already knew he was the historian, so he didn't interact with money in any way, which makes things remarkably less interesting." Brow crinkling in frustration, she continues. "Based on his social media, he didn't have any family drama, there's pictures of his wife scattered throughout."

With a humorless laugh, I add, "And you know if they were heading for divorce, they'd disappear from each other's social media." She confirms, "Exactly. I even cross referenced her social media and everything seems fine, no red flags." With a sigh of defeat, she starts closing tabs, and she must stumble on something interesting, because her eyes widen in a state of pure shock.

"Mma, mmmah."

I grab her laptop, angling it in my direction. Eyes widening, I finish for her, "Miniatures."

Chapter Twenty-Nine

Elle

C ohen and I share a look of mutual understanding. He speaks first, "So I really did go on a date with a murder."

"You just might've," is all I can manage. The crime scene photo stares back at us from my laptop. It's a shot of the food table with crime scene tape strewn across the frame. Sitting on the table with the assortment of dishes, is none other than a miniature. This is what we needed to place her at the scene. This proves Layla could have poisoned the mac and cheese. Maybe she left the miniature on the table after poisoning the dish.

I try to play devil's advocate. "Just because there's a miniature on the table, and she openly told you about her hobby creating said miniatures, doesn't necessarily mean..." I trail off, realizing my argument is falling apart the more I try to insinuate the opposite.

Cohen jumps in, "Yeah, because I'm sure there are tons of other people who had to work the Back 2 Cool Event because they're on the committee and create miniature diorama things for fun."

"Ok, no need for that level of sarcasm. I get enough of that from the kids."

Regret clouds his features. "I'm sorry, I didn't—"

I put a hand on his arm to stop him. "Cohen, don't worry about it. You've had your first observation, taught all day, and instead of being home, you're working on a case that we are out of our depth and can't solve."

He drops his arm, causing my hand to slide down. Right as I'm about to pull it back to my side, he grabs my hand, not letting go.

"You're wrong," he states with renewed conviction.

Thrown off and distracted, my thoughts are a jumble. "Huh?"

"We can solve the case. We literally try to motivate one of the toughest age groups every day. We can solve a murder case."

I hope he's right.

We walk in silence for a few minutes, giving me time to take in scenery on the way back to our cars.

I fidget with my purse strap. "So what now?"

"What do you mean?"

"Well, now that we know who the murderer is, what do we do?" I wonder in frustration. This seemed so much easier in the crime shows.

He glances my way with a conspiratorial smile. "We plan a trap."

CHAPTER THIRTY

Cohen

"E, I can't stop looking at it," I lament as I breeze past her, keeping a steady pace toward my classroom door, unsure of whether to stop or continue to my destination, so I opt for a middle ground, toy soldier style. I hear a small gasp and the click of her flats engage as she bounds after me.

"I told you not to look, Cohen." She sighs as she not so subtly nudges my shoulder trying to reach my desk before me.

Our conversation must sound interesting out of context as students give us looks fit for watching a circus act, as they zoom around us almost colliding, but not quite. I make my way to my desk and frantically reach for the mouse before Elle can slap my hand away. I let out a small yelp as she walks around to my screen.

"Cohen, I'm sure it's not that—"

"Ahh!" We both jump in unison as if a virus suddenly attacked our computer causing an animated monster to pop up on the screen while watching the dial tick in the wrong direction.

A few students turn around in their seats, but most just ignore us, completely used to our theatrics. This is what we so affectionately nicknamed the "Teacher Meter" which is a way for students to rate us on our overall teaching abilities and adequacy as human beings. Or at least, that's what it felt like, but the prompt was if students felt valued, which translated to do I like you or not in teenager. If the dial of death drops below seventy percent, you will find yourself sitting through sensitivity training to "reform" your bad behavior.

Let's not talk about what happens if you have two bad years in a row. I feel like I'm playing a bad game of hopscotch, constantly hopping from one foot to the other, but never truly gaining momentum. Respect me, like me, learn from me, but have fun, leaving me afraid to plant both feet on the ground, for fear I will lose my balance.

I hear a faint scratching sound as I look over and see Elle using one of my sticky notes to write something. She starts, "Since we only have a minute before the bell and don't have enough time for a true pep talk, look at this sticky note once I walk away. This is my first year Teacher Meter score. You will beat it, so you'll be doing better than I was. Don't focus on the meter, just focus on beating my score."

Before I have time to agree to the terms on this apparent sticky note contract, she turns on her heel and power walks back to her classroom right as the chime of the bell dings. Knowing I should be taking attendance, I quickly reach for the sticky note and my mouth hangs open.

The note reads... fifty percent. I know there's a story there that hopefully she'll tell me one day. I never would have guessed perfect teacher Elle ever had any doubts or shortcomings. I know she's mentioned a rough first year, but I always thought she was exaggerating since she's one of the best teachers in the building now. Maybe she wasn't.

With those thoughts swimming in my head, I start my lesson with a new confidence. Teacher Meter forgotten. For now.

Unable to put my curiosity aside, I walk into her room as the final few lingering students make their way to lunch.

Slightly out of breath, I'm at her desk as she turns to grab her lunch box. "Hey, so I have to know the story of your first year." She jumps in surprise, spinning around to face me. I cut in before she has a chance to speak.

"You're such a good teacher, I never believed it was as bad as you hinted at." She gives me a sad smile and gestures to the student chairs.

"Pull up a chair and I'll tell you."

Once I'm situated in the small student seat, she takes a deep breath, mentally preparing herself.

"Ok, so I was the definition of that overeager, doe-eyed teacher ready to change student's lives. I was so focused on creating games, classroom organization, and decorating my room, that I didn't put enough emphasis on lesson plans, pacing, and behavior management."

I want to reach out and hold her hand but stop myself. She squirms in her seat and continues.

"My mentor tried to warn me, but I thought she just didn't understand my teaching style. Anyway, it all came to head during an evaluation when a student had a meltdown during a formal observation and I didn't handle it well. From that point on, I lost control of my class, and it's next to impossible to get it back. Long story short, I got 'needs improvement' on my evaluation and got put on a performance plan. The teacher meter score where half my students agreed with my observer was the final straw in my confidence. Even though I turned it all around, I still remember the pit in my stomach when the admin would walk in the room. It might seem irrational, but sometimes I wonder if it's just luck that's helped me come out of it. I know it's weird to still be concerned with it years later, but it will take a while to recover from that kind of ego hit."

I'm stunned that she gave me such an honest, unedited version of what happened. "You know you took that and used it as fuel to help teachers like me not find themselves in the same boat right? That's pretty incredible," I muse, unable to hide the admiration in my voice.

She scoffs. "Thanks. I figured this would make you run the other way."

"I'm not running," I declare. A beat of silence passes between us as we push in our chairs and wordlessly walk over to join the others for lunch.

The crinkling of Herald's aluminum foil battles for attention over our conversation, prompting Brittany to side-eye him before raising her volume a notch. "So how many times has everyone checked their teacher meter?"

In between bites, Herald answers, "I don't check that stupid thing. They'll let me know if I have sensitivity training or not, so why go through the effort?"

"That's a good point. All day I've had it pulled up on a separate monitor, and it's done nothing but stress me out," Brittany admits.

"Exactly, don't sweat the small stuff," Herald advises.

"Your kids not liking you is the small stuff?" Elle asks, splitting her attention between Herald and her sandwich.

He grumbles, "Are they safe? Are they learning something that will help them later?"

She starts to answer, "Well, yeah—"

But he cuts her off, "Then you're fine. If you sweat all the small stuff, you'll burn out."

Brittany jumps in with a laugh. "And you're not burnt out?"

He retorts, "You try not being burnt out after 40 years of working with teenagers. I'm still here aren't I?"

We all acknowledge his response with shoulder shrugs and mhmms. No one is trying to start an argument today.

Brittany glances my way. "What about you, Cohen? Are you displaying your meter for the kids to see your 100% score?"

E jumps in before I can respond, "Lay off him, Brittany. Just because he's new, doesn't mean he's dumb."

I look down at my desk instead of directly at the other teachers. "Besides, I'm down to 95%."

I hear a few gasps, and Brittany laughs. "Oooh no. Who did you piss off?"

I look up in time to see the other teachers glaring at her and motioning for her to cut it out. They drop their hands quickly, in an effort to cover up their signals from me.

E continues, "Just because you're jealous of his shiny, new optimism doesn't mean—"

"I remember when I was optimistic. Those were the days." Brittany sighs.

Against my better judgement, I take the bait. "How long did it last?"

She smiles. "I got a good five years in." She looks straight at me. "But that was before Covid."

Everyone in the room nods in understanding. E and I are texting a side conversation to lay out the details of the killer trap, and it's making my head spin trying to keep up with two different trains of thought simultaneously. I put my focus on that, as we hash out our trap.

By the end of lunch, I survived more lighthearted mocking, and we finished our plan. I want to say that we deserve to remove the amateur in amateur sleuths, but I should wait until we see this plan through. Unfortunately, as a teacher, I've learned that plans change.

CHAPTER THIRTY-ONE

Elle

"And that's when I realized I forgot my SD card," a student recounts. I laugh at the ridiculousness of the situation, when I spot movement from the corner of my eye. Jade's red hair is pulled up in a high ponytail and gives a final swish as she stands in front of me.

She normally doesn't visit me during her conference period since I have a class. The fake smile she throws my way creates an instant pit of nerves brewing.

In an octave too high, she trills. "Heyyyy. I'm supposed to watch your class while—" The static of the loudspeaker crackles above us, causing every occupant's shoulders to rise in a collective jump scare. We really need to get that fixed. Principal Mitchell's voice fills the room, "Will Elle Dannon and Cohen Sinclair please report to the office immediately." A wave of irritation hits as I wonder why he couldn't just call our classroom phones and tell us to come down. The lunch group is never going to let this go.

I leave the room to a chorus of "Oooohs," from the teenagers apparently moonlighting as 5-year-olds.

As I make my way slowly down the hallway, another door opens. I hear a shuffle of footsteps and Cohen bumps my shoulder. Clocking my expression, he soothes. "It's nothing. We're fine. We're gonna be fine."

In a moment of doubt, I answer before I have time to mask my reaction, "Are we?" I challenge. I notice his fingers twitch as if he'd give anything to hold my hand in support. But since we can't, we just walk the rest of the way together in silence.

One of the buzzing overhead lights flickers in a constant rhythm fit for a horror film as we pass.

A sense of forebodingwashes over me, making me want to turn and run when we get to the principal's office.

When we enter his space, Mitchell's spine straightens and he clasps his hands, all business. A flashback to darker times tries to take over, but I shake my head in an effort to rid myself of that first year that follows me around like my own personal dark cloud. I glance at Cohen, so I don't have to make eye contact with the principal as we sit in the chairs facing his desk.

Cohen's posture has shifted—his back is ramrod straight, and his brows are furrowed together in concern. This layout feels more akin to an interrogation room than an office, but maybe that's by design. If I was a teenager, I would spill my guts with one glance from the principal.

He's the first one to break the silence, turning his attention to this monitor. "It's come to my attention that you two have been the subject of an Instagram account called." He adjusts his readers, leaning in closer to the monitor.

Hearing his monotone voice rattle off the handle sound infinitely more ridiculous, making me feel like a teenager being chastised by a parent. I'm unsure if this is a rhetorical question, or if we're supposed to chime in. Undeterred, he continues, "It seems they've captured several instances of you two canoodling, and it's become quite the distraction."

"Distraction for who?" I demand, trying to keep my voice steady. Yelling at the principal will get me nowhere.

"Everyone." Sighing, his mouth curves down into a more pronounced frown, "We've confiscated notes between students that are polls of how long you've been together, and there have been traffic jams in your hallway for the past two weeks."

Cohen chimes in, "The two aren't necessarily related. That could be a change in the—"

Principal Mitchell cuts him off. "Tardy slips have increased, from these fun detours."

Cohen gulps and I can see the fight leave his eyes as he slumps into his chair.

"So," he continues, "I'm going to need you to fix this."

"How are we supposed to fix this?" I question, disdain radiating from my body. Is an administrator really telling me I can't have a boyfriend? The double standards set on teachers never ceases to amaze me.

Already bored of the conversation, he turns back to his computer. "Well, I guess you'll have to figure it out."

I walk out in a daze, more enraged than shocked about having to once again figure it out without being properly equipped.

The walk to our rooms is steeped in charged silence. I feel Cohen's hand brush mine, but stop himself from holding it several times. I can tell he wants to reassure me, but we can't come out of a meeting about PDA holding hands.

The rest of the day passes quickly, and I zombie my way through the rest of my classes. Cohen texts to talk after class, and the pounding behind my eyes is an indicator I don't want to do this now.

After all the students have filtered out of the room, Cohen tentatively knocks and steps inside.

"Hey," he manages.

"Hey," I respond, drawing my eyes up to meet him. His hair is disheveled, and his sleeves are haphazardly pushed up, sitting at mismatching lengths by his elbow, and the other on his forearm. It's comforting to know he is as affected by that conversation as I am.

"Where do we go from here?" I ask. I take in a gulp of air before continuing my monologue before he has time to answer.

"After I was put on probation my first year, and I fought so hard to keep my job with help from my mentor teacher and all my colleagues, I can't jeopardize my job now that I'm finally getting the hang of things." I huff out in frustration.

Cohen's eyes widen as he is trying to figure out what that means for us. "I'm assuming that question wasn't supposed to be rhetorical, so I hate to put a blanket statement on it, but we'll figure it out."

I scoff and cross my arms over my chest.

"I know you want a concrete answer, but even though that was a setback, I think we can figure something out, because, well. We have to."

Incredulous, my voice jumps up an octave. "A setback? That was more than a setback."

He steps forward and holds onto my arms as if I'm a life preserver trying to float away. "Look, we're teachers, but humans too. Having a life isn't against the rules and I won't let you give up on us if your biggest concern is what admin will think."

He backtracks. "Unless after all this, you don't actually like me. Then who am I to stop you? I'll just shove my feelings in a box and pretend the kiss never happened." He takes a breath, as if steeling himself for a second monologue, and I hold up a hand to stop him.

"Even though it would be less messy if I didn't, I do like you Cohen." I sigh as I tap his foot with my own. "I think I was already looking for an out and when the principal got on our case for our stalkerazzi, I took it as a sign from the universe. But that would only make us miserable."

He pulls me in for a hug, and I wrap my arms around him. I open my eyes and notice a computer screen from a student who forgot to log out behind me. Abruptly, I break our hug as I notice what site is pulled up.

Cohen looks at me in confusion, until he notices what I've zeroed in on. We power walk towards the computer, determined to beat it from timing out.

"It's Anne. The one that talked to us at the haunted house."

Understanding passes over his features. "Ah, a member of your fan club. Don't you need to check your seating chart?"

"Seating chart?"

"Yeah, the map of where they sit." Cohen nods as if I'm asking what a lesson plan is.

I shake my head. "Oh Cohen, don't tell me you try to wrangle teenagers with a seating chart."

He straightens. "Yeah, all the books say it establishes order."

"For freshmen sure, but above that you're just asking them to disrupt the class trying to talk to their friends. You know what? Let's table this conversation for another day, but the chart has got to go."

"It's been Anne all along. I didn't see that one coming," I confess as we continue to stare at the Instagram account that started it all. There on the screen is the undeniable proof. Instagram, with our fan/ship account @TeamDannonSinclair.

"Me either." His eyes lock with mine. "So, what are we gonna do about it?"

CHAPTER THIRTY-TWO

Cohen

One minute I'm sitting at my desk, forcing myself to grade assignments before school, when I hear what can only be described as a cross between a squeal and a screech. I jolt from my desk and my feet carry me before I can form any more thoughts. The source is coming from the direction of Elle's room. I open the door loudly and my breath catches as I register the source of the commotion. Jade is holding the phone almost to Elle's nose. "What is this?!" She screeches, shaking the phone.

Maybe it was naive of me to think this would all blow over after our stunt, but I guess I was wrong. Elle smiles knowingly, and slowly pushes the phone out of her face.

"We figured we'd put the rumors to rest, so we can get back to our lives," she explains.

Jade recites the exact caption we crafted yesterday under the selfie we took in her room. We're both smiling at the camera, cheek to cheek. I move closer to E's desk, fully inserting myself into their conversation.

"We might be the focus of this account, but we've never told our side of the story. We've been dating for a little bit, but since it's early, we didn't want to jinx ourselves. We appreciate the encouragement, but we're teachers first, so please, stop with the paparazzi photos. School is for learning, not gossiping about teachers. We appreciate your respect moving forward to keep our private life private."

Jade takes in a gulp of air, still wide eyed. "This is huge! You announced your relationship to the entire student body. This account has more followers than we have students."

Elle and I both groan. We haven't analyzed it enough to come to that conclusion.

I speak up, "This was our first stop after alerting HR." I clear my throat. "One of E's students is behind the account, so we scheduled a post when she forgot to log out, and sent everything off to HR before it hit, so we're officially above board."

Jade gets between both of us and pulls us in for a group hug. "I'm so proud of you guys," she trills, squeezing us tight.

The rest of the morning is uneventful until it's time to meet Elle to talk to her student, Anne, about the account. We decided it would be better to talk to her together. Luckily, she's in fourth period, which just so happens to be Jade's conference period, so she's going to watch my class for a few minutes. Right on cue, I see a pop of red hair by the window as she knocks on my door.

She salutes me as we switch places, and I can't help but smile to myself, happy that Elle found a friend who cares about her as much as

I do. Even if that friend can be zany at times. Thankfully, she's more Phoebe Buffay than Janice Litman-Goralnick.

Elle is hunched over her desk, one hand on the trackpad as she submits attendance when I walk in. She turns at the sound, and I give her a quick nod. She catches the cue and calls Anne up to her desk. As she walks over, her eyes widen when she notices both of us waiting. Her steps slow as if she's debating making a run for it, but she persists, marching up to the desk, feigning confidence. "Hey, Ms. D, what's up?" She tries to play it cool, but her nervous energy is audible.

E motions to the hall, and the three of us step outside. Elle waits a beat to start for maximum effect.

"Well, yesterday we came across something interesting after school. A certain Instagram account was sitting on your computer after you came in last period to finish your edits," E trails off, giving off her best teacher look. Her teacher 'look' is so good, I'm gonna have to ask her for tips later. Even I'm nervous, and very thankful I'm not on the other end of it.

Anne cracks almost immediately, looking between us. "I'm so sorry. I didn't mean to cause any trouble. It started out as an innocent, fun little thing my friends and I started." She grasps her hands, eyes glistening.

Elle's eyes mirror hers, hurt etched deep in her irises. "But why? Why did you do it? What do you have against us?"

Anne gulps. " No! Nothing! I just want you to be happy. I knew that you wouldn't make the first move, and I wanted to give you guys a little nudge in the right direction. I never meant for it to get this far."

Elle pulls her in for a hug. Anne breaks and starts crying into Elle's sleeve. I make eye contact with E, and she nods, indicating I'm free to go. I leave the two in the hallway as I go to relieve Jade.

"How'd you do it?" Brittany asks between bites incredulously.

"Seriously, what teacher magic do you guys have?" Herald wonders.

Jade reads off the post from her phone: "This is the last post on this account. We set out to use our powers for good, and our work is done, and our ship is official."

This may be the first time I've felt like things were trending in the right direction lately. My observation results came back positive, this Instagram thing is finally over, and I even scored a 90% from the teacher meter. Now, if only we could make some headway in this case. Then everything would really be trending upward.

Elle just shrugs. "We found the owners of the account and talked them out of posting again."

Brittany sighs. "I guess I'm happy for you guys, but now I'm going to have to get my gossip from somewhere else. It was really entertaining."

I jump in. "You wouldn't be saying that if the account was focused on you."

Our conversation shifts as Jade changes the subject. "So, what is everyone doing for Thanksgiving break?" An upbeat chorus fills the room as everyone chimes in.

Being able to put school aside and just enjoy break is doing wonders for my overtired, overworked brain. I can practically smell the coffee as I march up to the front of The Plot Thickens. Elle and I have been spending more time together lately and that hasn't stopped during break. We plan to get some case work done and finish the final touches on our plan to catch the killer. For amateur detectives, we feel pretty confident.

The bell chimes and the boards creak under my feet as I step inside. I see familiar blonde curls already in our spot and a wave of warmth washes over me. It's not a feeling I'm used to and am determined not to take for granted. With the chaos of the case, I'm not going to distract us now, but once our plan has been put in action, I'll make my feelings known.

I hesitate. "Can we run it again?"

Elle sighs but agrees. "It has to be Layla. She creates miniatures which were literally at the crime scene."

I chime in, "And the misappropriated funds from the Scholars for Tomorrow scholarship have to start with her. She handles all the money."

She giggles. "Misappropriation of funds? Who are you, a school board member?"

"Shut up," I say through a chuckle. "Fine, embezzling from the scholarship fund."

She gasps as if she almost forgot the most important piece of evidence. "And the shoes."

I grimace. "But are we sure those belong to Layla? I don't think I've ever seen her in sneakers?"

"She knew she would be on her feet for duty the whole night, so she came in sneakers."

I huff, but she cuts me off before I can reply. "The rose gold sneakers tell us the killer is female. Maybe she didn't want to risk getting poison on her shoes?"

I mull that over. "I don't know, E. That still seems pretty thin."

"Sure, on its own it's thin. But when you combine it with the other evidence it's another thing pointing in her direction."

"Are we jumping to conclusions?" I ask.

"We might be. That's why our trap will draw out the person, and we can send Riley in her direction," she says with conviction, trying to convince me of its merit. Why does this feel like the fake date thing all over again?

"Do you really think he will take us seriously?" I ask lightly. Trying to be reasonable, but not upset her. I finally feel like we're on solid ground, and I don't want us to backtrack now.

"Maybe not with what we have now, but that's why this will give us something to go to them with and present our case."

"Or put a target on our backs," I point out, hoping I'm wrong.

"Or help the police solve the case like any good amateur sleuth. Cohen, why don't you sound as enthusiastic about this as before? Did something change?"

"You. Well, you and me," I start, slowly gaining courage as I continue.

"It just feels real now." I swallow. "And I don't want anything to happen to you. You're putting yourself in the middle of this and forcing our hand."

She reaches across the table and squeezes my hand in response.

"Ok, let's catch a murderer." Veronica Mars, eat your heart out.

I start, "Partners in crime," offering a fist for me to bump.

My knuckles tap with hers as she finishes, "All the time."

CHAPTER THIRTY-THREE

Elle

A nother day, another hallway conversation. I'm counting down the hours until our plan is set in motion after school and we may finally be able to put an end to this nightmare. If we can just figure out who poisoned Mr. Anders, then we can get some closure. And I can move on with my life, knowing his murderer has been caught. Cohen reminded me several times there's nothing I could have done to save Mr. Anders, but I can't help feeling like I owe him.

I was the last one to talk to him, and I can't help but think that if I realized the mac and cheese had been tampered with, then maybe I could have stopped him from eating it.

I jump as Riley bumps my shoulder. "Lost in thought?"

"When am I not?" I ask.

He laughs. "True, are you planning what game you're going to do next? What's left? You've already done everything." To most this would seem like a friendly inquisition, but Riley takes any chance he can get to complain about my teaching methods.

"How would you know?" I ask absentmindedly.

"I know because I can hear it from my room. Every. Day."

There it is. I bite back, "Hey, those games work. And weren't my certification scores higher than yours last year?" He scoffs.

Cohen walks up to my side. "Lay off her, Riley. If I had her class sizes, I wouldn't have to teach so many random graphic design sections. Clearly, the learning games work."

Riley laughs. "You're biased, but message taken. At this rate, you two will be married by the end of the school year."

At that, I hear a sputter and cough from beside me. I glance over and notice the travel mug in his hand.

A concerned student walking by does a double take. "Mr. C, are you ok?" She glances at me, eyes wide. "He's not dying is he?" Her friend pipes in, "Not another one." Raising their voice an octave as if he can't hear, they ask, "Give us a thumbs up if you're ok."

Cohen manages to give them the signal and chokes out between coughs. "Choked. On. My. Water." He slowly returns back to normal, slightly out of breath as he leans back against the wall. The concern on his students' faces was sweet. Everytime we talk about them, he acts like he isn't making any progress, but I can tell they genuinely care.

We have a clear view of Riley's classroom from his open door. In an effort to restore our conversation, I venture, "Riley, it looks like you could try a game or two, your students look bored to tears."

We all glance at the room. Several students have their heads down on the desks, and they're flipping through their police manuals with looks of pure boredom.

"Well, they can get used to it. It's not supposed to be fun," Riley informs us.

"I'm just saying, if you broke down the manual into sections, and worked on memorization exercises, you might improve test scores." I glance at Riley's less than impressed expression.

I sigh. "Fine, I'll drop it."

Tired of our conversation, Riley waves us off and returns to his room, shutting his door behind him, and locking out a few kids that were right behind him. They knock until Cohen unlocks the door.

When he gets back to my side, he glances my way. "Don't worry about him. I love your advice. It hasn't steered me wrong yet."

I laugh. "Expect for a certain outing with Layla."

He smirks. "No one's record is perfect."

With that, the minute bell rings and we make our ways to our respective classrooms.

CHAPTER THIRTY-FOUR

Cohen

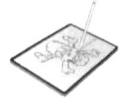

U gh. Nothing haunts me more than the tabs I have open on my laptop. They pop up rapid fire as I desperately try to navigate to my intended location. I'm about to close a photo that pops up right as my mouse hovers over the browser, when something catches my eye. I lean in closer to the screen, as if that will magnify the image, and zoom in. It's the crime scene photo of the food table from Back 2 Cool night. We stared at it until our eyes blurred the details. The details...

I suddenly notice something at the end of the table, half covered by the miniature classroom. The solid grey cashbox sits with a key hanging out of the lock. My gasp fills the space as I realize the miniature isn't a classroom. It's the PTA meeting room. Complete with a podium. A podium where a certain PTA president resides—

Elle's tinny voice fills my quiet classroom as she chirpily says, "Hey, Pat. I didn't realize the PTA was helping out tonight." Hoping for a better result than the restaurant, we're trying the phone trick again.

My heart drops to my stomach and I scramble out of my seat, flying into action. I almost run face first into an open locker.

Crap, Crap, Crap, Crap, Crap. I careen around the corner, my shoes creating squeaks and squeals that echo down the hallway, and I slip and slide my way to the cafeteria. I've never been so frustrated with freshly waxed floors. I don't even want to look back at the scuff marks I'm surely making. Subtly isn't any option. But none of that matters. Lives are at stake.

Specifically, my favorite person. Why did I think this plan would work? I knew I couldn't convince her otherwise, but I should've pushed harder. I reasoned with myself that Layla wouldn't try anything in a public place, but I don't know what Pat would do. He's not an employee, so he has nothing to lose. He could hurt her, and I'll have to live with knowing I could've done something to help.

I slow my steps in an effort to stay under Pat McPatterson's radar as I get closer to Elle. I continue to listen to their conversation in my headphones, simultaneously forming a plan to save E. We're not going down without a fight.

Chapter Thirty-Five

Elle

My hackles rise as I hear footsteps behind me and the classic sound of sneakers tripping on the cafeteria floor. This is it. Time to prove I can make it as an amateur detective. I pivot towards the noise dramatically, and visibly deflate, but try to keep my fake cheery disposition. False alarm, Layla isn't the one striding towards me, it's just Pat McPaterson.

"Hey, Pat. I didn't realize the PTA was helping out tonight."

He smiles. "The PTA is always willing to lend a hand."

My eyes lower to his shoes. His white sneakers. With rose gold details gleaming as they reflect off the fluorescents, projecting a murdery flair. His eyes glance down at his shoes, and he meets my gaze with a smirk. A sinister smirk that seems more ominous than his initial greeting. Well, we were dead wrong.

The whoosh of the heater turning on, and low hum from the lights rush into my ears as I become hyper aware of my surroundings. He takes a step closer to me, and I take a step back, trying to stay in our general vicinity. I hope my phone is still connected and Cohen's on the other end. That way I still have a chance.

"What are you doing here Pat?" I pause, deciding to go full scorched earth. "Really?"

"I was just trying to lend a hand. Like I always do. Like I've done for the PTA for the past two years." He starts shifting his weight but doesn't move any closer, clearly calculating what to do next while he starts his monologue. You know, the villain monologue. I really thought that was only a thing in TV shows, but every second he's talking, he's not killing me, so I'll take it.

"It's a volunteer position that I'm not compensated for."

Extra work beyond your job description you're not compensated for? Join the club.

"I got demoted at work a few months ago, because I wasn't focused on my day job. The school trip was coming up and I needed a cash advance."

"So you skimmed from the PTA scholarship fund?" I finish slowly understanding his motive.

"Yes."

"But didn't Layla catch you? She does all the books?" I ask incredulously. Why kill Anders when Layla seems like she should've been the victim?

He shakes his head, the smirk never leaving his features. "Not if you take it out of the cash box and hide the carbon copies of a few receipts before she does the final tally."

"And Mr. Anders caught you?" I venture.

"He was showing me some photos on his camera when I saw a picture of me in the background, sliding the cashbox away from the table. I couldn't let him post that photo. I knew once they're on the computer, I could never truly get rid of them. I needed that camera."

"So you poisoned his mac and cheese?"

"Yes, there were chemicals still in the janitor's closet from the take back toxic waste drive. I mixed it in the dish in a makeshift lab in one of the lockers. But I had already put some in his coffee earlier in the day, so the mac and cheese was just insurance that it would work. I didn't know how much I needed for it to work"

I reel back in disgust. "So now a boy is without his dad for the rest of his life and the future of the scholarship fund is in jeopardy because you wanted cash and killed to make sure no one found out."

He nods gravely, as if remembering I'm the only thing between him and getting away with murder.

In an effort to further distract him, I keep going. You can't multi-task while killing someone, right?

"How did you know we knew?" I correct myself to distract from the fact that Cohen's my partner in crime. "I knew?"

He laughs. "That Instagram account."

I sigh internally. I will literally never get away from that stupid account.

"There is a photo of you two making googly eyes at each other, and you have the crime scene board on your laptop and it says – Pink shoes. I figured you'd remembered my shoes and had been keeping tabs on me."

"But those are women's shoes," I stammer.

He breathes through his nose, whistling like a frustrated freight train horn. "They're. U-N-I-S-E-X."

"Whatever you say," I mumble.

I notice something moving in my field of vision and use my peripherals to clock Cohen's stature. He's behind Pat, out of his sightline. I'm careful to not look in Cohen's direction to give us away.

Static screeches through the air, alerting Pat to the walkie talkie I borrowed from the assistant principal's office and hid by the microwave table nearby as Plan B. I always have a Plan B.

We startle into motion. Pat dives at me, Cohen sprints my direction, and Riley power walks around the corner, gun drawn. Wait, does he carry that on campus? I swerve quick enough that Pat goes flying on the floor, looking as if he's trying to do a face first snow angel. Riley is on him in a second, handcuffing him. A whoosh of air leaves my lungs, and my shoulders drop to their normal position. My hands shake as the adrenaline flowing through my blood stream continues to pump, even as the danger subsides.

Cohen pulls me into a hug and I wrap my arms around him, hanging on tight. His hands rub my back in slow circles and I'm definitely getting makeup on his shirt, but we couldn't care less.

Later I'll fill Cohen in on everything. How I ran into Riley and told him about my plan to lure the killer, making sure he was on the other end of the walkie talkie, so he could be on standby too. It took a lot of convincing to get Riley to agree, but he decided being on standby for our stupid plan, his words not mine, was better than one of us getting hurt. Cohen and I thought that having Anne post a strategic photo on the ship account would lure Layla to the cafeteria, not realizing that Pat was watching us all along and caught the clues.

I could harp on the fact that we idiotically cleared the killer and didn't see him coming, but I choose to point out the fact that we set a one size fits all trap that ended up catching the person responsible. Take the win, where you can take the win. This is finally over and not only did Cohen and I make it out in one piece, but we actually helped catch a killer.

It can't bring Mr. Anders back, but hopefully it can give his son closure and keep anyone else from becoming the next victim at the hands of Pat McPatterson.

CHAPTER THIRTY-SIX

Cohen

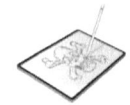

M y eyes are practically bugging out of my skull as I shut my car door, slack jawed. The town square has been transformed into a holiday wonderland.

"Amazing, right?" Elle says as she shuts her door.

Crap. I was so mesmerized by the lights, that I didn't notice Elle getting out of the car by herself. I was going to open her door. *Get it together, Cohen.* I nervously wipe my palms on my corduroys, grabbing my gloves out of the zip pocket of my coat, and meeting her at the front of my car. Not only is this our first real date—I'm not counting the disaster that was Laylagate—but I plan on asking E to officially be my girlfriend tonight.

We are technically HR official, but I never asked her specifically and I want to make things clear from the beginning of our relationship. It took so long to change her mind to act on her feelings for me, that I don't want another uphill battle if she regresses back. I look her way, and my heart naturally picks up its rhythm as I glance at her profile.

Her eyes are sparkling as she takes in the scenery, and my favorite smile is in full view.

It's her relaxed, wide smile that causes a matching one to take over my features. I grab her gloved hand in mine, feeling the muted warmth of her palm.

Elle breaks our companionable silence as we walk toward one of the shops on the square. It's already dark, the shop's soft, warm glow beckoning us forward.

"Having lived here all my life, I always forget to do this kind of stuff."

"When's the last time you came?" I ask, giving her hand a soft squeeze.

"Probably high school, honestly." She glances at the center of the square, where most of the lights are concentrated. "They've added a lot since then," she finishes wistfully.

She angles my direction. "Do you miss Dallas?"

I think for a minute. "Yes and no. I'm lucky my whole family moved up here, if I didn't have our Sunday dinners, I don't know what I'd do."

"You have family dinners every Sunday? Without fail? And everyone shows up?" she asks incredulously. "You mentioned them a lot, but I didn't realize they were every week."

"Yeah, it's a rule. My sister and brothers know you don't make plans Sunday evening," I say on a laugh. "One time, my brother had a date during dinner, and I thought Mom was going to disown him. I've missed so many this year, and I have the call history from my mom to prove it."

We both share a laugh, and I realize even the timbre of our voices meld together perfectly.

The door jingles as we step across the creaky floorboards leading into the shop. The overhead lights are off, and a soft glow radiates from the various lamps and candles lit throughout the space. A dark oak worktable sits in the middle, already loaded with supplies.

I lean close to E's ear, brushing her hair out of the way, to whisper in her ear, "Surprise. It's a cookie decorating class." She knew we'd be looking at lights in the square afterward, but I wanted to keep this until now. She's always talking about using the element of surprise to add whimsy in lesson plans, so I thought it could apply to dating too.

With an excited smile, she breathes, "This is so cool." She beelines towards the table to get started. Once she realizes I'm not right behind her, she glances back and motions for me to join her. I happily oblige.

The instructor demonstrates how to do intricate designs with the frosting on the Christmas sweater cookie, with confident precision. I watch in awe, wondering what my sad excuse will look like. We start setting up our workstations. I pick a plain stocking cookie with red sprinkles and icing, while Elle chooses the plain sweater cookie with a combo of blue, green, and yellow icing.

"I finished the books," I start.

Focusing on getting the base of the cookie covered, E distractedly asks, "What books?"

Bag of icing in hand, I turn her direction to give her my full focus anticipating her reaction. "The ones you recommended. *The Body-guard* and *You With a View*."

Almost dropping the icing bag in her cookie, she quickly sets it down and whips her head in my direction. "Wait, you actually read those? Both of them?"

I laugh. "Yeah, you recommended them to me. They're your favorites, right?"

"Yeah, they are. What'd you think?" She casually picks up the icing bag again, resuming the task at hand.

"I may even add Theo Spencer and Jack Stapleton to my book boyfriend list," I say just to make her laugh.

When a giggle bubbles out, I can't help but grin. "How do you know about book boyfriends?"

"My sister talks about them all the time. She has a color-coded list." I roll my eyes. I don't tell Elle about the presentations she has given in the living room on that very topic. I can safely say for my brothers and my dad, she could not have a less captive audience. My mom is the only one that tries to listen and asks clarifying questions that just prolong the whole process.

Maybe E could be a one-woman audience and they'd have such a great time discussing it, that we wouldn't have to sit through it at all. That alone could cement her status with my brothers and dad. They'd be eternally grateful. At the last one, we tried to start a paper football game by launching them off the couch cushions when she went to change the slide. She caught us, confiscated it, and added 30 more minutes onto our time.

"Why is it color coded?" Elle asks, enraptured by the methods of a fellow type A book lover.

"By niche and genre." Why did I know this? Ugh, maybe the presentations were more effective than I thought.

"Oh, that's smart." I can tell E is making a mental note to reorganize her list later.

"You two would really get along. You'll have to come to one of my family dinners soon." I try to slip in casually to gauge her interest.

She meets my eyes. "I'd love that. But are you sure you want me to meet your entire family?"

"My favorite person meeting my other favorite people? Yeah, I'm sure." I bump her shoulder in endearment, which causes her to lose control of the icing mid squeeze, and it lands right on the instructor's apron as she walks by.

Elle's jaw drops as a result of our bad timing, "I'm soooo sorry."

The instructor laughs. "You're fine. That's why we wear aprons," continuing her rounds and scooping the frosting from her apron with one finger to conduct a taste test.

I can tell by the flush of her cheeks, that E's still embarrassed, so I lightly rub small circles on her back and lean in to whisper, "I should be the one that's embarrassed. I ruined your creative process on our first date." A soft laugh squeaks through even though I can tell she's trying not to draw any more attention our way. She angles towards me, in an effort not to be overheard. "Seriously. Try to suck less." A breathy laugh escapes me, surprised by her call out. We both start laughing harder, not caring if we're heard by the instructors and other patrons.

Determined to keep her mind moving in another direction as we get back to our cookies, I start, "So when you were in high school, were you the person that did everything on group projects?"

She stops mid sprinkle dusting, crystals still between her fingers and looks at me. "Why do you say that?" The arch of her eyebrow tells me she's playing along and not genuinely offended. Yet.

"You just seem like the kind of hardworking, perfectionist, who can't risk a drop in assignment quality." I gesture towards her cookie which is almost done and could rival the instructor's. It has a green base, with blue stripes and red accent berries mixed throughout.

"You're not wrong," she finishes with the sprinkles before continuing, "I bet you were the one person who loved group projects because you could get someone like me to do all the work." She gestures down at my barely iced cookie. *Touché.*

In mock offense I answer, "I got better in college, but in high school, yeah, you're spot on."

We chat back and forth easily for the rest of the class. Once our creations are complete, the instructor takes a photo of us holding our cookies on my phone and a polaroid camera. I snatch the polaroid before Elle.

"Hey, what if I wanted that?" she questions.

Tucking it in my pocket, I text her the photo from my phone. "Here's your photo, but the polaroid is mine."

"Fine, but the next one is mine." She extends a pinkie my way. I agree to the terms via pinkie promise, and glance at the photo as she heads to get our coats. She's smiling at the camera holding her cookie out with pride. I'm holding my cookie, but looking and smiling at her. I didn't even realize I did that, but apparently this shop can add candid photography to their list.

Once we're all bundled up, we start making our way back to the square. The hub of glowing lights draws us closer like procrastinating students to *Cool Math Games*. Walking hand in hand, I try not to think about how deeply I hope this is the first date of many.

As we draw closer, I notice the intricacy of the lights that must've been a huge undertaking for the setup crew.

"I wonder how much the town's electricity bill increases this time of year," I ponder out loud.

"That's such a guy thing to say," she jokes with a laugh. "Forget about the bills we don't have to pay and just take in the magic. This is basically a Christmasy art exposition."

I apply her advice, taking a second look, putting logistics aside. Mis-matched colors create patterns, covering every surface. Every tree trunk, branch, and even the plants in the flower beds are aglow with a rainbow of Christmas lights. There's a certain magic to being surrounded by lights, from the ground to the trees curving over our heads. A grid of lights connects the trees, creating a glowing canopy. She gives my hand a squeeze, propelling us forward.

I take control, slowly leading us in the direction of my next surprise. I can see the white lights of said surprise up ahead. E's too busy taking it all in to notice. I stop suddenly at the end of the line, and Elle almost runs into me from the extra momentum. She puts her free hand on my back, shifting over to my side again, never letting go. She stands on her tip toes and leans to the side, trying to investigate, but the line is wrapped too far for her to see.

"What're we waiting for?" Her brows scrunch together in confusion.

I smile, giving her hand a squeeze. "Want to go on a carriage ride?"

Her face lights up, eyes shining bright with the reflection from all the surrounding lights. "Yes please!"

CHAPTER THIRTY-SEVEN

Elle

C ohen never ceases to surprise me. The cold is starting to seep through, despite my ultra thick layers, and honestly, I'd take lunch duty by the band hall for a year if it meant a cup of hot cocoa right now, but none of that matters. I'm about to go on a carriage ride with my date.

Maybe about to was too strong, the line was moving so slow we'd probably be here for at least the next 30 minutes. I gently yank on Cohen's hand, to pull him down so he can hear me despite the mix of noise from the whistling wind, crowd of jolly patrons, and Christmas music playing from tinny speakers overhead.

"I'm so thankful we're alive to do stuff like this." Cohen's features turn serious, and I notice a flash of leftover fear in his eyes as I remind him of our recent brush with death.

"Did I tell you I saw Riley the other day?" I wonder aloud, knowing I hadn't gotten there yet.

"No, where?" he asks, fully invested in the direction of this conversation.

"At the school yesterday," I confess, hoping if I speak quickly, he'll let it go.

I have no such luck. "E, on a weekend? What was so important you had to go up there?"

The biggest change they don't tell you about when you go from being alone to having someone care about you, you see your habits in a whole new light.

I brace for his reaction. "There was a cabinet that I knew I wouldn't get to organize next week with all the chaos before break."

"Elle, that sounds like something that can wait," Cohen suggests, looking at me knowingly.

"I know, I'm trying to be better. That doesn't happen overnight." He nods in agreement allowing me to continue, "So, Riley was telling me that Pat's verbal confession gave them the information they needed to connect the evidence from the photographs, and they even found a locker where he mixed the poison. The fork with mac and cheese sauce was still there and everything."

"Someone finally found a use for the lockers," he says morbidly.

"I had the same thought." She nods solemnly. "They are running the finances to confirm that he was embezzling from the Scholars of Tomorrow fund under Layla's nose, but it looks like he'll be going away for a long time."

"What about his son?"

"I asked that too," I say, smiling at our similar train of thought.

"He has an aunt and uncle in Florida that would love to have him," I explain.

Cohen nods sympathetically to the news. Innocent kids having to uproot their lives is never ideal.

"Since when does Riley ever voluntarily give you that much information?"

I shrug. "I guess he felt bad about my near-death experience and wanted to make it up to me. I'm not about to question his methods. I want the insight."He laughs. "True. I just can't believe our PTA president murdered a parent just to keep it a secret." Cohen shakes his head incredulously.

I commiserate, "Yeah, I guess it just shows the lengths a parent will go to make their kid happy. This all started because of money for the stupid school trip."

"So this didn't make you want to quit teaching, right?" I ask nervously, afraid of putting a seed of doubt in Cohen's mind.

"No, not at all." He shakes his head. "I'm looking forward to next semester. Imagine the time we'll have without a murder to investigate. That sounds like many more date nights are on the horizon." He smiles bashfully.

"Now, that I can get on board with," I agree. Having been caught up in our conversation, we were lulled into the steady rhythm of stepping forward, only for me to realize we're next.

Once the couple in front of us boards the carriage, Cohen leans back down a bit, so we can continue our conversation. "There's some rules for this carriage ride."

"Like what?" I ask, interested to hear what he has in mind.

"No talk of murder, work, or anything school related." He grins.

"Deal," I agree without hesitation.

With wide eyes I take in the carriage. Wrought iron covered in a tangle of white lights, it's mocked up after the iconic Cinderella carriage, round pumpkinlike shape and all. A horse dawning jingle bells hooked to his saddle waits at the ready, steam from his breath emanating in the freezing air. A friendly coachman waves us forward so we can board.

We quickly take the blanket set out and scoot close together. Cohen wraps an arm around me, allowing me to feel the warmth of his body heat on one side.

"So, what's it like having a roommate that doesn't have a winter break? Is Ren jealous?"

"Oh no, he thrives on routine. I'm sure it will be quiet during the day, but after this week and all the chaotic energy at school, I think I'll need it."

"One more week."

"One more week," he echos.

"Hey," he starts slowly. "I have this plan to ask you something and I want to do it before our carriage ride is over."

"Sure, what is it?"

"From the first time you almost ran me down trying to get a lunch duty slot," she laughs in remembrance, "to all the days we've spent talking in the hallway, working at The Plot Thickens, and everything in between, I've come to the realization that I have feelings for you."

"Well, I hope so. You've already kissed me and we're on a date right now."

"Yeah, but I want to take it a step further."

"Which is what?" she clarifies.

"Will you be my girlfriend?"

"Yes!" she answers without hesitation.

CHAPTER THIRTY-EIGHT

Cohen

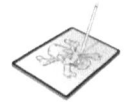

I take the opportunity to kiss her before I say something stupid. More stupid than that whole monologue. If the smile on her face is any indication, she doesn't care that it wasn't as smooth as I anticipated. I'm sure to the average passerby, we look like dopey idiots who chatter excitedly and openly stare at each other the rest of the ride, but I feel like I'm still in shock.

I have been mentally preparing myself for the worst, and hadn't considered the better option, so now I'm basking it in.

I quickly shoot a text to my mom as the ride comes to a close, to let her know I had some news at family dinner this week. I did see them at Thanksgiving, but I am making family dinners a priority. A long overdue priority. As I put my phone back, I noticed Elle putting hers away too.

"Who'd you text?" I wonder.

"Jade, I said I'd fill her in. You?"

"My mom. She likes to know if we have news to share each week, so she can pester us about it," I explain.

Smiling, she gives my hand a squeeze. "I'm honored you consider this big enough to share."

"Oh yeah. And there's no use trying to hide it from my family. They'll pick up on it instantly, so I've learned it's just easier to be up front. They're going to be so excited, you'll probably get an invitation from my mom instantly."

The carriage comes to a stop, and we start on our mission to get back to the warm car. A feeling of hope radiates through me. When I nervously walked into my classroom that first day, I never thought I would run into a certain blonde genius who would have me begging to be the other half to our sleuthing duo.

My elbow almost lands in the salad dressing pushed to my side of the table as I reach for another breadstick. The table is full of food, as per usual, and it's a minefield to miss knocking over a dish, candle, or floral arrangement. The heater is whirring, and the table is dark except for the glow of candlelight. For the month of December, Mom gets into the Christmas spirit, and to her that means candlelit dinners. My dad just goes with it, and my brothers always complain it's impossible to see their food, while my sister loves the ambience. Phones are not acceptable light sources at this table, and with all the work my mom puts into these each week, she deserves to be particular. I glance at the faces around me.

Mom is at one end while Dad is at the other, they share small smiles when they catch each other's eyes as if they haven't been married for years. Zach, the oldest, moves lettuce around his plate, lost in thought. Jesse shovels pasta into his mouth as if it will disappear if he doesn't finish fast enough, and my sister Molly is only a few years older than me, though she acts as if she's the youngest, but that spot goes to me. She's complaining about something to the table, but I tuned her out a few minutes ago.

I'm about to interrupt her, but before I can start the announcement, my mom beats me to the punch.

She claps twice—our universal signal to shut up, and all eyes are on her. "Cohen texted me he had some news to share, so he'll start us off tonight." I can count on my fingers how many times I've volunteered news at family dinners in the past, so the admission has everyone intrigued. They're all perked up, leaning my way, and I have so much eye contact from them it's unnerving.

Is this what it would be like if my entire class paid attention at once? Hmmm, guess I'll never find out. I clear my throat in an effort to stall. "A few days ago, I got a girlfriend."

My mom and sister squeal and the rest of the table erupts in cheers.

"Finally, it's been forever," my sister kindly points out.

"Who is she? How'd you meet? When are you bringing her to dinner?" Mom asks, already starting on her interrogation.

My sister whips out her phone, momentarily forgetting the rules. My mom's too laser focused on me to notice.

Molly gets both thumbs at the ready, "So what's her full name? And can you spell it?"

Jesse swallows his bite with a loud gulp. "You guys need to chill."

Zach nods. "Give him a chance to breathe."

Realizing they'll keep at it until I answer a few of their questions, I start, "Her name is Elle, and she's a teacher at Wilson." Mom and Molly share a quick glance, motioning for me to continue. "Our classrooms are almost right next to each other, and we met when she almost flattened me in the hallway trying to get a lunch duty spot."

I can tell by her expression that something clicks into place for Molly. "Wait. Is she the mentor that was helping you?"

Mom waves her fork in circular motions midair. "She helped you with the bulletin boards we saw in your classroom when we saw your room, right?"

Molly sighs. "Ooh they looked professionally done."

Zach scoffs. "A professional classroom decorator?"

Molly volleys. "Oh come on, you've heard of weirder jobs. It could happen." She shrugs.

Snapping back to me with laser focus, Molly continues, "Sooooo? What do you like about her?"

I could tell she was getting impatient with my bare minimum answers, but I want Elle to be able to make her own first impression without any priming from me.

I sigh, knowing she won't let this go, even though it's embarrassing to recite my girlfriend's best attributes to my family. "Well, if I had to choose my favorite things about her, one would probably be her charisma. She may seem quiet and serious at first, but if she's in front of friends or students, she captivates the room. Watching her teach makes me feel like I'm doing it wrong.

She's driven and works harder than anyone I know. And she's a great listener. When you talk to her, you feel like you're the only one in the room."

Mom and Molly look at me with smiles and slightly glassy eyes, and Jesse chimes in, "Yeah that's great. But is she hot?" That earns him twin glares from both women, but he ignores them, waiting for an answer.

"Yeah, of course." This earns a shoulder bump and hums of approval from Jesse and Zach on either side of me.

"Found her!" Molly triumphs waving her phone around.

"How?" I ask, in shock by the speed of her cyber stalking. Maybe we should've added her to our crime solving team. I shake the thought away. Then I would've received texts at all hours from my sister with "important" information. Pass.

"She's the only Elle in the teacher directory on the school's website." Zach and Jesse make a move to push back their chairs to come look, but Molly holds up a finger.

"I'll drop it in the family group chat." Seconds later, our phones are pinging and I glance at Elle's face staring back at me. This feels like a weird invasion of privacy, but that's par for the course with us.

"She teaches audio/video production, and her classroom is adorable!" Molly muses to the table, eyes close to the screen. Jesse taps my shoulder and shoots me a thumbs up, trying to stay under Molly and mom's radar. He leans in and whispers, "Does she have any friends?"

"Her best friend Jade has a boyfriend, sorry."

"Jade, hmmmm," Jesse mumbles to himself. Shrugging, he suggests, "Maybe they'll break up?"

"Anything could happen I guess," I concede.

Mom grabs her readers and throws her own rules out the window, holding her phone up to get a better look. "She's very pretty, Cohen. And she has kind eyes."

Jesse snorts, getting marinara on the tablecloth. "She's not a dog."

"Huh?" Mom looks taken aback. "I never said she was."

Zach intervenes, "Kind eyes does sound like a thing I've heard people use to describe animals."

Molly chimes in, "What are you even saying right now? I've never heard that."

Jesse asks aloud obnoxiously, "Is the phrase kind eyes used to describe animals?"

Mom shakes her head in exasperation.

Jesse recites, "It's used to describe both animals and humans. Smiles can be deceiving, but since eyes are the window to the soul, kind eyes are a thing." He smirks. "So I'm right."

Molly glares at him. "We're both right. Humans AND animals."

Zach, always the peacekeeper, tries to quash the argument, "Everyone's right, so drop it." He sighs. "Cohen, you might want to give it a few months and make sure she really likes you before you introduce her to all this." Mom makes a noise in protest.

"Yeah, I think you're right," I say as we share a look of acknowledgement.

Jesse laughs. "This family hasn't had the best track record once significant others meet us."

Dad interjects, "Don't put that on us."

Molly's deep in thought. "Wait, you're right. There was Emma—"

"Did her hair ever grow back?" Jesse wonders.

Zach pauses, considering it. "Hmmm, I don't know. We don't talk anymore."

Molly continues, "And Todd."

Jesse replies instantly, "Todd sucks."

We nod in agreement.

Molly concedes, "Yeah, he did kind of suck."

I snort. "Kind of."

"Everyone else in my friend group had a boyfriend. I wanted one, ok? And he was available," she replies defensively.

"Wonder why," Jesse mutters just loud enough for her to hear. She's about to raise her voice in protest, but I swoop in, "Jesse, it sounds like you're forgetting about Rhonda."

The table says, "Rhonda," simultaneously. There's an undertone of disdain from everyone, except Jesse, whose tone sounds too wistful for my liking. The best way to describe Rhonda was like Rachel Berry from Glee reincarnate.

Hyper competitive, in your face, and lacking the ability to chill. She drove us crazy, but Jesse was entranced.

Zach points out, "But I have a girlfriend."

Jesse smirks. "For now. When are you bringing her to family dinner?" Zach opens his mouth to argue, but mom jumps in, snapping, "I don't know what you're talking about. We're a delight." She smooths her napkin on her lap, punctuating her point.

The table erupts in laughter. Even Dad joins in.

CHAPTER THIRTY-NINE

Elle

"Freeedom!" Jade screeches as we all check the last item off the list. Cohen and I cover our ears as we stand in his classroom, staring out at rows of freshly pushed in chairs and powered down computers.

Before we can officially leave for break, we have a chore chart style to-do list of items like turning in grades, cleaning up, unplugging stuff to save the school's utility bill—the works. We've been staring at our lists the past week, and it's the only thing standing between us and Winter break.

Grabbing her bag, Jade says in her best patronizing mom voice, "You two have ten minutes to say your goodbyes and meet me at my car, E."

"Cohen, I'm sure I'll be seeing more of you during break," she says, winking at me, and I can feel my cheeks take on a rosy hue.

"You know it," Cohen finishes for her.

Jade leaves the room and Cohen steps closer to me, taking my hands. I break into a smile, looking up at him, opening my mouth to speak, when the jarring jangle of someone yanking the locked door handle fills the space. With a sigh, he reluctantly goes to the door and opens it slowly.

Principal Mitchell steps through the door, looking sheepish. If he's here to scold us for holding hands when there aren't any students around, I'm more than ready to defend us.

Without a greeting my way, he stammers, "I'm glad I caught you. Cohen, I just got off the phone with the principal at Wilson West."

Even though his back is to me, I can hear the confusion in his tone. "The high school across town?"

"Yes, we have a new CTE director who will be in charge of the Career and Technical Education classes throughout the district."

Hesitantly, Cohen asks, "Ok, why did you have to find me specifically?"

The principal takes a big gulp. "The graphic design program just received a large grant. Up until now, the classes have underperformed and coaches who need an extra prep are given the class, so it's become a free for all. With this new funding, they want to bring someone in with industry experience that can turn it around. And the district wants you to be that person."

There's a beat of silence, before he answers, "Wow, I'm honored to be asked. If I accepted, when would I start?"

Mitchell laughs uncomfortably. "January."

"Of next school year?"

He wipes his hands on his pants, and I'm shocked his teeth aren't chattering. "No, this January."

I suck in a breath. He's literally a first-year teacher. How can they move him in the middle of the school year? I walk up behind him and put my hand on his shoulder. As if by instinct, he instantly brings his hand up to cover mine.

"We're going to have to talk it over." He glances back at me. My heart warms at his lack of hesitation to include me in decisions despite our relationship being so new.

The principal's face falls, as if he was hoping for an instant acceptance. At least he takes it as his cue to leave, mumbling his goodbyes while backing out of the room.

Once he's gone, we glance at each other, mirror looks of panic, excitement, and shock cemented on our faces.

"Well, that was…"

"Yeah. So what are you going to do?"

"I don't know what we're gonna do." He shrugs unbothered, as if he's deciding what to bring for lunch, instead of the trajectory of his future, and subsequently the future of our relationship.

As if he can sense the thoughts swirling in my head, he grabs my belt loops and tugs, so I'm facing him. "But we'll figure it out together."

Unable to hide my grin as I stare with what must be googly eyes, I recite, "Partners in crime."

"All the time," he chimes, matching my level of enthusiasm.

"Is that less cheesy yet?" I question with a smirk. If Jade heard our catch phrase, she would probably gag from the sheer level of lameness.

"Shut up," Cohen says in a laugh, breaking our hold to scoop up my teacher bag. He grabs my hand and shuts his classroom door, dragging me with him to go drop me off with Jade in the parking lot. Well, winter break just got a whole lot more interesting.

I could start freaking out about how much next semester is gonna be weird without Cohen down the hall, a murder to solve, and who knows what else. But for now, I'm just gonna enjoy my winter break with my new boyfriend.

To be continued...

To find out Cohen and Elle's decision, be on the lookout for book two in the Teachable series. For the latest release updates, follow along on Instagram @whereileftoffpod or @kristenbahlswrites.

Acknowledgements

Thank you readers for taking a chance on my debut! Your excitement gave me the push to self-publish and I appreciate you more than you know! More Cohen and Elle is on the way soon.

Thank you to Cassidy, Ally, MiKayla, and our book club. I appreciate your support and excitement! I can't wait for more of our writing sessions where we always get each other off track. Thanks for being the best book club and friend group!

Thank you to M.K. Williams. Your guidance and support were invaluable! I admire you as a writer and friend and I would be bumbling my way through without your advice. You always went out of your way to answer everything and your mission to help authors everywhere is a testament to your character.

Thank you to Shayla Dugan. I don't know how to thank you for all the advice, laughs, pep talks, and feedback. Hopefully I can create characters as iconic as Ida, Juniper, and Gabbie! I've learned so much from you and I'm so glad we found each other. I'm looking forward to crying at the next piece of writing you put in front of me.

Thank you to Sarah Blair. I would not survive without our daily Polos. From my podcast guest, to critique partner, and everything in between, I couldn't have done this without you! Whether we chat for

5 minutes or 5 hours, I always walk away feeling lighter. I'm so lucky to call you my friend!

Thank you to Harriet Ashford, Staci Hicks, and Sarah Blair (again). Book Besties! Our group chat always makes my day and it's so fun to have other author friends to talk to on a daily basis. All of you amaze me with the way your champion and cheer on everyone around you. I'm so glad we all found each other.

Thank you to Dr. Melissa Dymond. Your advice, recommendations, and kindness don't go unnoticed! Your encouragement gave me the confidence to pull the trigger on publishing, and your support means the world.

Thank you to Alexa Martin. Thank you for talking through my plot documents and giving me insight that shaped the trajectory of my story. Your expertise gave me the confidence to start writing!

Thank you to my Beta readers, Paige, Jocelyne, Maheen, Ezrela, Shayla, Whitney, and Savannah. I can't thank you enough for taking the time to not only read my book, but provide feedback. Your comments helped shape the story and I'll be forever grateful.

Thank you to the 100 Covers team. As the first impression readers form about a book, I was so nervous to have my cover commissioned. Everyone treated my book with care and created an amazing design. I can't wait to see what you create for book two!

Thank you to Hungrydamyart. The chapter illustrations were such a fun, custom detail that added so much to the layout of the book. Thank you for bringing my characters to life in the character art. It's surreal every time I glance at the framed picture of them in my office.

Thank you to Ramona (@Proofreadereditor). You're the only person whose read through my book almost as much as I have. Thank you for your attention to detail, and comments that helped me hone the story into what it is today. You were a dream to work with!

Thank you to Jess (@ChapteronePA). Not only do I appreciate you squeezing me in, but being able to relax, knowing you would catch anything I missed after reading through it too many times on my own was invaluable. I'm so fortunate to have you in my corner!

About the author

Kristen Bahls is a Texas native, who's been a bookworm since birth thanks to her mom, the librarian. Even though she's no longer in the classroom, as a third generation teacher, she enjoyed her time helping students in Audio/Video Production.

When she's not writing, Kristen hosts the bookish podcast,"Where I Left Off." She's also trying and failing to meet her reading goal.

To get the latest on upcoming releases find her on social media @kristenbahlswrites and @whereileftoffpod.